STARLET

DANGER SLATER

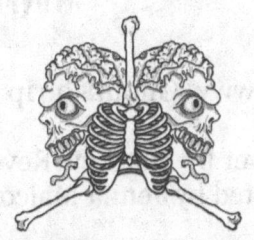

Ghoulish Books
San Antonio, Texas

Starlet
Copyright © 2024 Danger Slater

First Edition

All Rights Reserved

ISBN: 978-1-943720-98-9

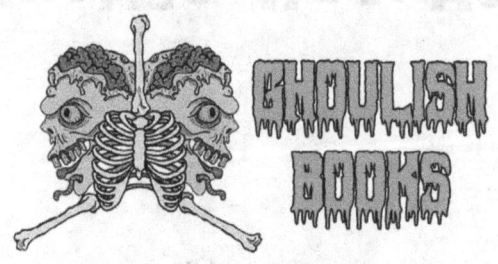

www.Ghoulish.rip

Cover by Matthew Revert
Edited by Jenna Malcolm

ALSO BY THE AUTHOR

Moonfellows
House of Rot
Little Miss Apocalypse
Impossible James
Puppet Skin
He Digs a Hole
I Will Rot Without You

CHAPTER ONE
THE PERFECT GENTLEMAN

(2003)
DIR. BY FRANK LATHAM

CHAPTER ONE

THE PERFECT GENTLEMAN

" . . . though festival buzz has been mainly centered around the gorgeous cinematography and impeccable production design, the real highlight for this reviewer came by the way of Brandon Bowers and his breakout performance as the titular Perfect Gentleman. Though a relatively new screen presence, Bowers delivers a masterclass in nuance unto himself, single-handedly elevating this already-tense indie thriller into something truly sublime . . . "

HE TOWERED OVER Canal Street in Carlsbad, New Mexico and haunted the highways that surrounded Kingsport, Tennessee. We knew him before we *knew* him, it turned out—his familiar and welcoming visage a mainstay on billboards and ad campaigns across the USA. From border to border, and coast to coast, in places like Greenville, Aspen, Marfa, Dubuque, Boise, Pensacola, Colorado Springs, Cheyenne. Name a city, name a state, and there he loomed, nearly 50 feet tall, a benevolent god watching over the morning commute, his polished white smile doing its best to convince you that you could buy your way into a better life, if only you owned a Rolex watch, or a Lexus car, or were drinking a cocktail made with Martini & Rossi extra dry vermouth.

Driving by, you might've once wondered who that handsome fella was, with his square jaw, and blond hair, and blue eyes as delicate as robin eggs. In a few years you would know the answer to that question. We all would. We'd be seeing his name on marquees and magazine covers the world over:

BRANDON BOWERS IS THE PERFECT GENTLEMAN

Maybe you weren't a fan of his films. Or maybe you were.

Bereft of the everyman appeal of Harrison Ford, the surprising range of Brad Pitt, the unfettered commitment of Nicolas Cage, or the emotional gravitas of Tom Cruise, Brandon Bowers had no need to rely on these tumbledown archetypes. Brandon Bowers possessed a star quality unto his own. Alluring yet masculine. Approachable yet aloof. Magnetic with just a hint of darkness beneath it. A roguish kind of charm. A bad boy kind of flair. He looked good in an Armani suit. He looked good on the silver screen. Our eyes were drawn to him, our collective attention at his command, we were but tiny rays of light continuously collapsing into the center of his seductive black hole, an allusion certainly not lost on Déjà Seawright, because before she ever met him—before she even moved to LA—she'd been transfixed by Brandon Bowers and his indefatigable smile too, beaming at her from the posters in the lobby of the movie house in downtown Eau Claire.

Déjà tried her best to hide her accent these days. Bit her tongue every time it snuck up on her. That Midwestern drawl, the specter of her past.

"That's an interesting little vocal inflection you have there, Ms. Seawright," a casting director would say to her if they happened to catch it. "Where did you say you were from originally?"

"Eau Claire."

"South France?"

"Wisconsin."

"Oh, sure. Middle America. The Heartland. Or is it the Rust Belt? Either way, it's Springsteen country, right? I'm a big fan of The Boss."

"I thought he was from Jersey."

"Huh? Might need to double-check you on that."

Déjà didn't begrudge anyone for not knowing anything about Eau Claire. If she hadn't been born there, she wouldn't have known anything about it either. Heck, that was the reason she came to Los Angeles in the first place. To flourish beyond her provincial roots. To branch out in a way she couldn't back home. To become a "real" actress. To finally shoot her shot. To go to audition after disastrous audition. To explain basic American geography to a bunch of fully-grown and ostensibly intelligent adults. To apologize for her twang, for her too-fizzy hair, for her slightly disproportionate hip-to-height ratio, for the color of her skin, which depending on the production was always too dark or too light. To live in The Valley, in a crappy old apartment building on the verge of condemnation. To work at a shoe store in order to make ends meet. To eat microwave ramen most nights because she couldn't afford anything else. To keep on hustling. To follow her dreams.

Yeah, things had been tough this past year, but life wasn't all doom and gloom. There were moments of reprieve that occasionally graced her. A commercial shoot here and there. A fun (and alcohol-fueled) night out with like-minded new friends. The weather was great, generally speaking, and the tacos were to die for. Such as it was, just enough to keep her going.

And, of course, she couldn't deny the little electric thrill she still got whenever she passed by an advertisement for the latest Brandon Bowers feature, her heart going pitter-patter in her chest in much the same way it did nearly a decade ago, when she was just a teenager, and in much the same way it did, once again, when she met Brandon in the flesh for the very first time.

Joe Peeps on Magnolia. Loud and hot and perpetually overcrowded. The best pizza in The Valley, at least according to those who claimed to be experts on such things, so it was a popular spot for both tourists and locals alike. It had something to do with the water they used to make the dough, which Déjà had been told they flew in from Catskills every other week. That was their Magic Ingredient. Their Special Sauce. Their 11 Secret Herbs and Spices. A unique blend of minerals that could only be found in the rivers and reservoirs of upstate New York.

Not that any of that mattered, in the end. As far as Déjà's palate and pocketbook were concerned, they might as well have been ladling their water out of a slop sink in the back. The food was cheap and delicious and you could get it by the slice.

There was always a line at Joe Peeps, and Déjà was standing in it, looking at the framed photographs on the

graffiti-tagged walls. For such a no-frills pizza joint they'd
certainly seen their fair share of celebrities. Frank Zappa.
Geena Davis. Emma Stone. Steve Buscemi. Grumpy Cat.
That dude with the braids from *NSYNC. Anyone you
could think of. Over 40 years in business and still going
strong. A neighborhood institution.

She'd been on her way back to her apartment in Van
Nuys after another doomed screen test. She'd starved
herself for two days leading up to it, burning off the last
little fold on her tummy that appeared whenever she sat,
and yet, despite being as camera-ready as she possibly
could, Déjà could tell by the look on the producers' faces,
the way their eyes wandered as she read, the subtle
collective glance they all shared the split-second she was
finished: she never stood a chance.

We'll call you and let you know, she'd been told. But
she'd already learned the lingo. She knew exactly what that
phrase really meant. They smiled at her, thanked her for
her time, and waved goodbye as she left. The people in this
city were always so polite, even when they were stomping
all over your hopes and dreams.

So, Joe Peeps to the rescue. The only surefire cure she
knew for the post-audition blues. Pizza like a band-aid.
Like a salve for her soul.

He must've come in just a few steps behind her. The
bell above the door chimed but she was too wrapped up in
her own head to notice, mentally dissecting the audition
over and over again. If only she said her lines *this* way
instead of *that* way. If only she stopped eating three days
ago instead of two.

She sensed his presence before she saw him.
Something in the air around her changed. A pressure drop.
A barometric shift. He was a stormfront sweeping into the
pizzeria. Hurricane Brandon. Category Five.

"Hey look, it's me."

He pointed to the photograph next to her. A candid
shot at least 20 years old. Probably taken with one of those

crappy disposable cameras everybody used before smartphones became a thing. There stood a young Brandon Bowers, early in his career, holding up a pepperoni slice in front of the counter, the flash too bright, washing out all the whites, turning his pupils bright red as the light bounced off the back of his eyes.

The Brandon Bowers of today was even more handsome. His voice was deeper in real life than it sounded on the big screen.

Her jaw fell open. Brandon stifled a laugh.

"Here, lemme get that for you, little darling." With a thick yet gentle finger he guided her mouth back shut, a not entirely unwelcome gesture, even if it was a little bold. "Hmm. You look familiar. Like I've seen you somewhere before. You don't happen to be Déjà Seawright, do you? The actress?"

Déjà couldn't help herself. Her jaw fell open once more.

Leftover Parts. That was what he recognized her from. One of the few gigs she'd gotten since she moved out here. And it was a promising one too. Until it wasn't.

Bowers was signed on as an executive producer, she knew that when she got cast—the "new Brandon Bowers series" they were calling it in the trades, although from what Déjà could tell from her one day on set, beyond his namesake, he wasn't actually involved in the production at all. Hands-off, simply an investor—a *famous* investor— carrying the kind of cache the showrunners could use to secure the rest of the budget.

The premise of the show was to give the viewers at home an allegorical and hyper-stylized glimpse into the sometimes-petty, sometimes-cutthroat world of international hand modeling. Sorta like *The Neon Demon*. Except with hand modeling.

HBO was interested and ordered the pilot, and after a

month of grueling auditions, Déjà finally nabbed the role of Matilda Speck, best friend to the main character, Lorna Ortega, played by the *Wizards of Waverly Place's* own Selena Gomez.

Déjà had only one scene in that first episode, filmed in less than six hours on the Warner Brothers backlot. But despite the brevity of her appearance, the director made it implicitly clear that her character was supposed to be the "moral center" of the entire show.

"You are the voice of reason," he said to her before the cameras rolled. "Lorna's conscience. The angel on her shoulder. You can see things as they really are, yet lack the power to do anything about it directly. Instead, you must subtly guide Lorna and try to light her path, despite her constantly pushing back against you and your sage advice. Is Matilda frustrated because of this? Of course she is! But she cares about her friend, and deep down she also knows she's Lorna's only olive branch, her final chance at redemption, the last tenuous thread still connecting Lorna to her life outside of hand modeling."

Déjà did her best. She delivered her lines with passion and aplomb. She imbued Matilda with all the raw humanity she could conjure. And she fucking nailed it. She could feel the character inside her, dancing with her bones.

HBO ended up passing. Not compelling enough, was the verdict. All flash and no fire. Déjà never even got to see the finished product. But Brandon Bowers apparently did. And now luck brought them into this pizzeria together. What were the chances?

"You were hypnotic, Ms. Seawright," Brandon said to her.

"Déjà." She tucked a lock of hair behind her ear.

"Of course. Déjà. No smoke, you were the highlight. The network execs even said it. 'This one's a supernova, bound to blow up soon,' they said to me. And I wholeheartedly agreed. And maybe *Leftover Parts* wasn't the vehicle to let the rest of the world know it, but believe me, little darling, your time is coming." He pressed his fingers to his temples and closed his eyes, taking on the mock affectations of a prognosticator. "I can *feel* it."

The big Italian dude behind the counter passed Déjà a plate with three gooey slices, dripping with cheese. She chuckled, cheeks flushed, embarrassed.

"Weird, I didn't order all this," she unconvincingly said.

"Nonsense. If you're hungry, you should eat." Brandon leaned past her, toward the man. "I'll have three cheese slices too, Gino."

He turned back to Déjà. Gave her a wink.

"That's real kind of you, Mr. Bowers," she said.

"Only parking lot attendants call me Mr. Bowers. Please, call me Brandon."

That was over a month ago now, and in the ensuing weeks, their relationship had escalated quickly. She and Brandon were developing a rapport. A friendship. A *flirtatious* friendship. Perhaps even a little bit more.

She followed him on Instagram. He followed her back. He liked her pictures. He viewed her stories. It was all so new. So unexpected. So exciting. Goosebumps ran up and down her arms every time he'd slide into her DMs. That little blue checkmark next to his name. Verified status. *Thee* Brandon Bowers.

This had been their main method of communication. Text messages. Snapchats. The occasional Zoom call over a spotty Wi-Fi connection. He'd been away on a shoot since the day after they met. Somewhere in Central Europe, he said. Liechtenstein or Luxembourg or one of those other odd little countries out there nobody knew anything about.

"I'm playing a samurai warrior who returns to feudal England after being marooned in the Orient some years prior," he told her. "It's an action film, of course, but it's got a lot of style. A bit Kurosawa meets . . . um . . . feudal England, I guess . . . "

Communicating electronically actually made things much easier for Déjà. It kept her from getting flustered. Gave her time to think about her replies. To choose just the right words. To craft the perfect comeback. To come across as either witty or coy, depending on how she was looking to tempt or tease him. And in doing so, she was able to rise above her schoolgirl crush and actually let her guard down a bit. Let the "real" her shine through without melting into a puddle at his feet. And, in turn, she liked to think she was getting to know the "real" him as well, the sheen of celebrity between them disappearing in the flurry of late-night notifications blowing up her phone.

"I can't wait to get back and see you," his message said.

"I can't wait either," her message replied.

"Think I can get a little taster in the meantime?" he asked, smirking purple devil emoji, prayer hands emoji, eggplant emoji.

"A taster?" Detective emoji.

"Don't be shy." Playful tongue out emoji. "Daddy's hung-wee."

So she sent him a few nudes. Nothing too lewd. More erotic than explicit. A quick photoshop to smooth out the blemishes on her skin, and into his inbox they went.

And, of course, Brandon sent a few back her way. Him without his shirt on, glistening post-workout. The pubic stubble like a clear-cut forest, just below his belt. A closeup shot of his small, wrinkled dick pressed up against a cold piece of marbled raw beef.

"Is that a London broil?" she asked as she looked at the photograph of his shriveled manhood laying atop the slab like a mealworm lost in a vast pink landscape.

"Little darling, this is filet mignon!" he replied.

She should've guessed. Like Brandon Bowers would be caught dead with anything BUT the finest cuts from the best butcher in town.

STARLET

A video popped up in her DMs. She clicked play. A shaky self-filmed clip of Brandon inserting himself into a slit in the meat and pumping away, muttering "fuck you, you little whore" over and over and over again, until he finally came all over the thing—a voluminous and iridescent load—roughly seven seconds after he started.

"So what am I supposed to make of all this?" Déjà asked.

Val regarded her with wide, beseeching eyes as she sucked on the straw of her fountain soda until she slurped it dry. "I think you might need to show me these pictures. Ya know, so I can judge for myself . . ."

The two ladies were sitting at a table in the outdoor food court at the Sherman Oaks shopping plaza where they both worked. Val wasn't employed at the shoe store like Déjà, but at the high-end purse shop next door. The two of them had met at the dumpster one evening as they were both taking out the trash. They shared a quick cigarette and became fast friends.

"Shut up. Just use your imagination, okay?" said Déjà.

"Mmm." Val sucked on her straw again.

"Val, c'mon. Stop messing around. I need some real input here. He's coming back from Europe next week and he already invited me to his house for dinner and drinks out on the veranda. I don't even know what a 'veranda' is."

"Dinner and drinks. Mmmhmm. I've heard that line before."

"This meat thing, it's weird, right?"

"Well yeah, of course it's fuckin' weird, Dé. But he's a big star. It kinda comes with the territory. You know Richard Gere used to put gerbils up his ass, right?"

"That's just an urban legend."

"Dé, one of 'em *died* up there."

"Would you stop?"

Val leaned back in her chair and ate a french fry. "All

I'm sayin' is, these people? The rich and famous? They're not like me and you. And I don't just mean because they don't hafta work retail. People like Brandon Bowers are a different breed altogether."

"What do you mean?"

"Look, the dude's been in the limelight for almost two decades now, so maybe he just needs a little extra *something-something* to get his motor running, if you know what I'm sayin'. Hey, I ain't one to judge, as long as it's consensual. And it *IS* consensual, isn't it, Déjà?"

"Yeah," she said, eyes darting to the left and the right. "I mean, it might not be what *I'm* necessarily into, but yeah, I haven't told him to stop."

"Well there ya go," said Val. "Just don't forget you're in the driver's seat, Dé, so you either gotta get on board or get off the ride. There is no place for in-betweens. Though for the record, I just wanna say, if I was in your position, we wouldn't even be having this conversation. This is Brandon Bowers we're talkin' about. You just won the hot guy lottery. I mean, I don't wanna influence you or tell you what to do, Dé, but at the end of the day, you're probably lucky it's ONLY raw meat play he's into and not some illegal pedo shit. These Hollywood types can be real freakshows, ya know?"

Déjà nodded. "Yeah. Yeah, you're probably right. Though I don't care how famous I get, you'll never catch me rawdogging a T-Bone steak."

Val laughed. "Never say never."

And on her way home that evening, Déjà thought about what Val said. Perhaps this was a bit of an *unconventional situation*, and perhaps in the bedroom Brandon Bowers had some *unconventional tastes*, but nobody got to the top by sitting on the sidelines and playing it safe. Déjà knew this instinctively, even from a young age, and while all her friends back in high school were busy getting knocked up by their methed-out boyfriends and starting their careers at the local Walmart, she was staying focused. Plotting her escape. Keeping her eyes on the prize. Hollywood was calling, and Déjà Seawright was going to answer. It wasn't enough to just be an *actor*. She wasn't going to stop until she became a *superstar*.

And Brandon was beautiful and famous and had a million connections all over the industry, and she figured if he had a few kinks that needed to be indulged in the process, then so be it. She was on the verge of something grand, and Brandon Bowers was her ticket inside.

"I wanted to talk to you about some of the projects I got coming up," he messaged her. "I think there might be a part or two you'd be good for. You're still gonna have to audition, of course, but I can at least get you talking to the right people. You got a real marketable kinda look, a whole young Halle Berry type thing going on, if you don't mind my saying so."

"Of course I don't mind you saying so," she replied, even though she'd long grown tired of that worn-out comparison. It was the same one everybody used, from her first drama teacher to her last casting call. Like there was only one light-skinned black girl anybody knew.

"Good," he texted her back, followed by a winking face. "Now send me a picture of you shoving a turkey leg inside of yourself . . . "

CHAPTER TWO

HOUSE OF SECRETS

(2005)
DIR. BY DAE-JUNG KWAN

"... *Bowers is again able to strike the perfect balance between pensiveness and pathos, proving that he is not only becoming one of Hollywood's most recognizable faces, but a serious talent to be reckoned with.* House of Secrets *is easily among the best of Kwan's American films, and in a true star-making turn, Bowers is the glue that holds the whole thing together. In this reviewer's opinion, it would be a literal crime should award season roll around and not have this performance among the Academy's top contenders ...* "

HER LYFT CUT off the 101 and made its way through the needlessly complicated and cartoonishly designed roads of the Hollywood Hills, toward the address Brandon Bowers had given her, somewhere in Nichols Canyon.

Left and right, up and down, around hairpin turns and past dead-end streets; this part of LA was a mystery to Déjà Seawright, who sat alone in the backseat, watching the sun disappear along the western horizon.

She spent most of her time in The Valley, either at work or in her rundown apartment at the noisiest end of Van Nuys, where it seemed like every single one of her neighbors was an aspiring actor of some kind. They were all so attractive and young and hungry. It was a regular *Melrose Place* out there. At any given moment you could lean out the window and hear impassioned snippets of out-of-context conversations—mobsters threatening informants, bosses admonishing employees, couples back-and-forthing melodramatically, damsels in distresses letting out bloodcurdling screams—people rehearsing scenes of every ilk, their voices in the night an incoherent chorus.

The Hills were quiet, though, and Nichols Canyon was the quietest among them. As her driver let her out in front of the Bowers gate, the silence felt almost oppressive. No police sirens. No music blasting from car stereos. No stomping feet pacing around the apartment above her. The houses out here were huge, ornate, and original, with sprawling fenced-off yards to keep them all separated, postmodern plantations dotting the landscape like a well-manicured beard.

Downtown Los Angeles was visible in the distance, high-risers blinking on and off like Christmas lights. A little over a mile away, at the bottom of the mountain, sat Hollywood Boulevard and all the iconography therein.

Grauman's Chinese Theatre. Madame Tussauds. Whisky a Go Go. And, of course, the apex of it all: the Walk of Fame. In her neighborhood all she ever saw were strip malls and chop shops. The *real* La La Land beckoned to her now from below.

It was brisk out for LA. The October wind took the heat out of the air and embraced her shoulders like a cold hug. Some days it was easy to forget that this all used to be desert. Other times, like tonight, the city was hellbent on making sure she remembered.

So she might've been slightly underdressed for the weather, but she certainly wasn't underdressed for the occasion. At least in this instance, form came before function. She had to look good. Look her best. A slender, low-cut top with a tiny glimpse of her toned midriff separating it from the flouncy short skirt—pink, her favorite color, puffed out like a tutu—resting just above her knee, showing off the shape of her muscular legs.

Just a peek, Mr. Bowers, Déjà thought. *A tease.* Though who was she kidding? She had a pretty good idea of how this night was going to play out. It was, in essence, why she was here in the first place and not meeting him at some restaurant or in public somewhere. Sure, she was coming in with a *tiny* bit of an agenda, but so was Brandon. And so was everyone else in this town, for that matter. Before the evening was through, they could both get what they wanted.

A tiny clutch held her cellphone and some lipstick and a few emergency tampons. She hadn't started her period yet, but she could feel it coming on, probably within the next day or two, like a hand between her hips, ready to wring her out.

She bought this outfit special for tonight. Val helped her pick it out. Accessorized and everything. It was beyond her meager budget, of course, but Déjà thought of it more as an investment than an extravagance. The only article of clothing she wore that she'd previously owned was the faded jean jacket she brought from Eau Claire to LA, which she now slid into like a security blanket. Pins over the left breast: the Bride of Frankenstein, a raised BLM fist, one that simply read LET ME PET YOUR DOG. The jacket looked ridiculous and didn't fit the rest of her ensemble at all. But it had personality. And it felt *elemental*, in a way. The last scrap of her old life she still held onto. Important somehow.

Heels clomped against the pavement, echoing throughout the empty street. Déjà reached the gate. Tall, wrought-iron bars on some kind of electric hinge, the only opening in the 10-foot-tall stucco wall that surrounded the property. Pikes stuck out of the top like it was some kind of medieval rampart. Unless you were in the driveway looking up, the entire house was hidden from view.

She reached out for the callbox built into the wall, but before she could press the button a voice hissed in her ear.

"Psst. Hey."

She looked around. Saw no one.

"Over here. In the bushes."

Stepping out from the shadows of a nearby sagebrush came an older man, maybe in his late 40s. Skinny. Sickly. Sweaty. In a Tommy Bahama shirt and khaki cargo shorts, looking about as inconspicuous as a diaper would be on the Statue of David. Déjà wondered how he had managed to camouflage himself so well.

"What the hell are you doing in the bushes?" she asked him.

He smiled at her. Wiggled his eyebrows lasciviously. "Going to see Brandon Bowers, eh? You his new hot little dish? His flavor of the week?"

What little hair he had sat glued to his forehead and his milky pupils darted back and forth, lizard-like. He licked his lips.

"Ugh, get outta here, you fuckin' creep," Déjà said.

She turned away from him, but he reached out after

her with an innocent and open palm. "Hey wait! Déjà Seawright. That's you, ain't it?"

She froze. Spun back around. "Do I know you?"

His disquieting smile widened. "No. But I know youuuuuuu."

"Look, buddy, I'm gonna call the cops if you don't tell me what the fuck you're doing out here, right now."

He held up a camera. A Nikon D850, with a bulbous flash attached to the top and a long, phallic telescoping lens sticking out from the front. The whole apparatus hung from his neck by a worn-out leather strap. He seemed proud to be showing off his gear, presenting it to her the way a catalog model might, holding the position for a few seconds longer than necessary, just to make sure she got an eyeful.

"I'm an independent contractor," he said.

"Oh. Paparazzi." She let out a small sigh of relief.

"Whoa, there, honey, we don't use the P-word anymore, thankyouverymuch." He snapped a quick picture of her. Point. Click. The flash temporarily blinding them both. She instinctively tried to cover her face, the way she always saw movie stars doing in the supermarket tabloids, though truth be told, she was simply playing the part. It actually excited her that someone *wanted* to take her picture. She did her best to suppress the smirk crawling its way across her face.

"I'm pretty sure you're trespassing . . . "

"Benny," he introduced himself. "And this is the street, okay? Public property. By order of the City of Los Angeles and the Great State of California Civil Code section 1708.8, I am well within my rights as a private citizen to stand here as long as I please."

"Whatever," Déjà said. "Just . . . stop taking my picture, okay?"

He raised the camera and snapped off another quick shot, blinding them both again. She huffed and gave him a stern look.

STARLET

"That was the last one. Promise," he said. "So what's the deal, huh? You and Bowers an item? Coming over for a li'l nightcap, perhaps?"

"I think I'm supposed to say, 'no comment,' here?" Déjà replied.

Benny chuckled. "Hmm. Well 'no comment' certainly comes loaded with its own bundle of *implications*, now don't it?

"'No comment' means 'no comment,' Benny."

"Ouf. Savage."

She hit the button on the callbox. *ooweeo oweeoowoo* it chirped.

"What are you doing skulking around in the shadows, anyway?" she asked the ~~paparazzo~~ independent contractor as she waited for Brandon to buzz her in. "How did you know who I was?"

"Oh, I don't know . . . " He motioned to the moonless night, no clouds above. "Just something in the air, I guess."

"Zen and the Art of Invading People's Privacy?" she said. "Is this how you get your rocks off, eh? Stalking celebrities outside of their homes?"

Benny laughed. "No, I get my rocks off on Thursdays when Mistress Veronica comes over and sits on my face. This here is more of a . . . *symbiotic relationship*, I suppose you could call it. Like a remora on the belly of a Great White."

"You're calling yourself a suckerfish?"

"Yeah, and your boy here is the shark."

"If this relationship is so mutualistic, then what does he get out of the deal?"

"Whaddaya think, lady? Fame is a helluva drug. And I'm the dealer. I keep him in the cultural conversation. I'm how Brandon and the folks like him stay relevant."

"You might be giving yourself a little too much credit."

Benny pshawed her. "People only have as much power as you're willing to give 'em. And stardom is a two-way street. So I'm not the parasite in this equation. Quite the opposite. I'm the one who is feeding *him*. We're *all* feeding him, to one degree or another. The only difference between me and the rest of the unwashed masses is that I was just clever enough to figure out how to get paid for it along the way."

The callbox made a beeping sound.

"Déjà, my dear. Right on time," Brandon's voice finally crackled over the speaker. Then a slight pause. "Hey, Benny? Benny, I know you're out there . . . "

Benny cast his eyes to the ground, cheeks gone red, looking like he'd just got caught trying to sneak a cookie before supper.

"Yes, Mr. Bowers?"

"Get the fuck outta here, Benny. Leave Ms. Seawright alone."

"Sure thing, sir," Benny said as the speaker buzzed and the gate swung slowly open on its rusty hinges. Déjà took a step onto the property, but before she left Benny called her back. "Hey, wait one last thing . . . " He reached out and handed her a business card.

BENJAMIN TEMPLESMITH: PHOTOJOURNALIST followed by a phone number.

"That's my cell," he said. "You see anything interesting in there, snap a picture and send it my way. People always want to know what's going on behind closed doors. We can even go splits on the sale. Make a small mint. Either way, beats working at the mall, amiright?"

Déjà slipped the card into her bag and walked up the driveway as the gate creaked closed and locked behind her.

Glass and concrete. Dutch Wood and steel. The exterior of the mansion was a work of modern art, made up of a set of protruding rectangles and squares, chunky fractals somehow giving birth to and consuming one another at the exact same time.

STARLET

The yard was neatly manicured. Hedges had nary a branch out of place. Green grass lay thick and immaculately trimmed. Déjà couldn't see them but Brandon warned her he had a few free-range peacocks roaming the grounds. "Just don't let 'em sneak up on you," he texted her that afternoon. "They can get a bit protective of their territory."

The driveway was curved, leading up to the portico extending from the front door, where Brandon Bowers already stood framed within.

Broad-shouldered and apricot-skinned, the California sunshine had turned his complexion a pallid and permanent shade of orange. 20 years in the industry and he'd barely aged a day, the living template for a leading man. Pretty, yet virile. Generic, yet puckish. Brandon Bowers, as handsome as he ever was. Perhaps even more so, if such things were possible, waxing *into* his looks instead of waning *out* of them. Here, he appeared before her as she'd envisioned him as a teenager. Godlike. Superhuman.

He held out his arms and Déjà slid into them like they'd been carved out of alabaster and contoured just for her. A kiss on the cheek moved quickly and smoothly over to her lips. Before she knew what was happening, his tongue was already in her mouth. She was instantly drunk on his touch, drunk on the moment. Subsumed by Brandon, totally, happily. Even the smell of him was intoxicating—not quite the chemical stink of cologne, nor the funk of an unwashed body. He smelled sweet. Redolent. Raw. Like he used one of those hippie crystals as a deodorant stick and somehow it actually worked.

Brandon pulled away, a string of saliva still connecting their mouths. Déjà fanned herself. "Why hello, Mr. Bowers!" She gave him her best imitation of a southern belle, muddled by her incurable Midwestern accent.

"Well hello there yourself, Ms. Seawright," he replied. "I take it you found your way over here alright? I woulda sent my driver to pick you up, but apparently today is his daughter's Bat Mitzvah?"

"No worries. It was a nice ride regardless. I've never been up this way before. It's beautiful. The houses. The view. Very secluded too."

"That's the idea." He winked. "Sorry about Benny, though. The dude is obsessed with me. He's like a cockroach. I can't seem to shake him."

"An occupational hazard, I assume?"

"Yes, it certainly is. Among other things . . . "

He planted another obscene kiss on her lips, which she reciprocated in full.

"I've been waiting a damn month to do that, you have no idea," he said. "And, might I add, you look ravishing, little darling. I could just eat you up. Mmm mmm."

She placed a hand on his chest and teasingly pushed him back a step. "Well a few thirsty DMs is one thing, but now that I'm here, it's a different ballgame altogether. Don't think it'll be so easy. I still have to be wined and dined."

He chuckled. "Oh, we're playing hard to get? On my front steps, no less?

"Guess I got some tricks up my sleeve, too," she said as she slipped by him into the foyer.

Immediately, the house opened up. Ceilings high above. Marble tile underfoot. An austere spiral staircase sat off to the side, leading to a second story, and whatever bedrooms and bathrooms and offices lay above.

Déjà looked around, already in awe. The lighting was soft, inviting, drawing her further in, only undercut by the odor that hung in the air around them—bleach or some other kind of astringent, that soapy hospital smell, sharp upon her senses.

"Shoes off, if you don't mind," he said. "They're lovely

STARLET

heels, but I just had the floors cleaned, as you might be able to tell."

She stepped out of her shoes, Brandon eyeballing her toes, licking his lips, chest heaving in and out, ever-so-slight, as if the sight of them stole his breath away.

She recalled a videochat they had a week before, where their flirting had reached a fevered pitch. It was dark out for both of them, though it was early in the morning for her and late in the evening for him. Sunrise and sunset. And still, charm radiated from him like the glow from a hearth. He kept her warm from a half-world away. They talked about everything during these calls, where she grew up, what her home life was like, her aspirations as an artist and a performer, and:

"God, if you were here right now, you better believe I'd be suckin' on them toes!"

"Brandon!" She laughed, scandalized.

"It's true! I'd be licking the dirt from right between 'em, if you'd let me. Nibbling on the ends, one after another. Just bite, bite, bite, until all your little tootsies were gone. I'd eat your whole feet so that they were just two stumps on the ends of your ankles . . . " His hand went down his pants. She could hear the rustling of fabric, the jangle of an undone belt. "You'd never be able to leave me. You'd have no legs because I'd have eaten them both. I'd consume you, my darling, little by little, one gentle sup at a time. Drinking your nectar. Savoring every last drop."

"Heh . . . er . . . um . . . that might be second date stuff you're talking about there, Brandon." She was getting uncomfortable, and he could tell. Mercifully, gentlemanly, he abated.

"I just think you're great," he said. "And I wanna get to know you, Déjà. All of you."

"Good," she replied. "Because I'd really like to get to know all of you too."

And now here she was, in his house, the man himself once again lusting after her feet, as promised, like they were the appetizer to the rest of her body.

DANGER SLATER

A door opened and closed from somewhere down the hall and a maid approached, a doughy middle-aged woman, with the smallest of wrinkles in the corners of her eyes and a single shock of gray in her shoulder-length hair. There was no sense of warmth or charity on this woman's face. To Déjà, she bore an uncanny resemblance to her own mother.

The maid had on a short jet-black frock with a white apron tied around her waist and she was carrying with her a large silver platter.

The maid stopped next to Déjà and thrust the tray at her. Eyes moved to her heels, slight curl of disgust on her lips. She motioned to the platter and raised her brow. It took Déjà a moment before she realized what this person was asking.

She bent down and picked up her shoes and placed them on the tray. The maid put a lid over it, and a half-second later, pulled it back off again. To Déjà's surprise, her pumps were gone. Replaced by a single piece of paper and a fancy fountain pen.

Déjà looked at Brandon, confused. "What's with the magic show?"

"That's just my housekeeper, Imani. She's a bit . . . theatrical, I suppose you could say. But she's very loyal, which is the important part, almost like family . . . "

Imani cleared her throat and shot Brandon a quick, censorious glance.

"Oh, right. Sorry. Not Imani. *Alice*. She insists that I call her Alice while she's on the clock. Like that housekeeper on *The Brady Bunch*, I guess? Though the dress is all wrong with the French maid thing she's doing. I told her she could wear whatever she wanted, but she insisted on the whole classic getup. Some people are just committed to the bit, ya know? Funniest part is, it's not even a real maid's uniform. I think she found it in my closet on her first day? One of the costumes left over from when we were filming *House of Secrets*."

"Where are my shoes?" Déjà asked him.

"No shoes in the house, ma'am," Alice interjected. "Those are the rules."

She thrust the platter forward a second time. Déjà picked up the paper. It was covered in writing. A lot of small print. Legal mumbo-jumbo. She gave it a quick perusal.

"Umm . . . what the hell is this, Brandon?"

"It's just a standard NDA," he said. "Very by-the-book. Nothing indecent."

"An NDA?"

"A non-disclosure agreement."

"I know what NDA means. I'm just wondering why you're having me sign one?"

"I know. I know. Not quite the height of romance, is it? But it's nothing personal, Déjà. I have all my guests sign them. If my grandmother stopped by for a visit, I'd have her sign one too. You saw Benny out there. Being in proximity to me can make people sometimes act all outta sorts. Everyone is looking to get a piece. Fame. Money. What have you. And I don't blame them. If I was in their position I'd probably be looking for the same thing. I'm just covering my bases, legally-speaking."

Déjà signed the contract and placed it back onto the tray. Alice continued to stand there, unmoving.

"She's gonna need your cellphone too," Brandon said.

"What?" asked Déjà.

"Again, it's not you. It's the system. Last thing I need is someone sneaking pictures of me in my own home. I'm sure you understand. But not to worry, Alice will keep your things safe until you're ready to leave."

The words of Val replayed in her head. *You're either on board or you're not. There's no place in between.*

She took her cell out of her purse and placed it next to the NDA and Alice once again snapped the lid shut over them, this time giving her a sly little wink before scooting back down the hall, toward wherever hole-in-the-wall she initially came out of.

"Good. Good. Now that *that's* out of the way . . . "
Brandon stepped over to Déjà, but instead of taking her
into his wide arms, he nodded down. Déjà's eyes followed.
His fly was already unzipped and his stumpy little wiener
was poking out of his pants like a mushroom spore.

She was taken aback, but only for a moment, and the
firm yet tender hand he placed on her cheek let her know
this was all perfectly normal, perfectly fine.

She reached out to touch him—to touch *it*—but before
her skin pressed against his, he froze, shuddered, hitched
his breath, and muttered 'oh shit oh shit oh shit oh shit'
right before splooging directly into her open palm.

Oily and bountiful and smelling faintly of the sea, the
load he almost instantly shot seemed to have a strange kind
of sheen to it, reflecting back the light of the foyer in pastel
rainbows. Déjà looked around for something to wipe her
hand on and, finding nothing, brought it to her mouth and
licked her fingers clean like they were covered in cake
batter. It tasted horrible, like rancid bay shrimp, though
she tried not to let her expression show it. Brandon
watched her and nodded with approval.

"So how about a tour?" he chirped when she was done.

Déjà kept pace with Brandon, like a patron at a museum
following a guide.

"You could probably tell from the outside that I had the
whole place renovated after I moved in," he said. "Razed
and rebuilt. Not just the exterior but the interior too. I
know there are a lot of people out there who might consider
such measures profane. They look at Hollywood like it is
this sacred place. Like every building and every street
corner has some kind of story to tell. I guess they think that
by honoring the history of this town, they'll be able to crib
a little bit of the magic of it for themselves. They'll buy
some crusty old mansion and say something like 'oh Clark

STARLET

Gable used to live here back in the 40s' or 'this place is modeled after Jayne Mansfield's Pink Palace' or whatever that case may be. But not me. I'm a self-made man, as I'm sure you could appreciate. I make my own magic."

Brandon led her into the immaculate kitchen, where not even a crumb could be found on the floor. The smell of disinfectant lingered in here too, even more pungent than the foyer. But the granite countertops shined and the stainless steel refrigerator hummed. Light fixtures hung from the asymmetrical ceiling, suspended above the island in the center of the room, with dinette chairs on one side, and a cast-iron gas range on the other. It was a sleek room of mercurial design, with three blank doors oddly lined up next to each other along the far wall. Déjà thought it looked like something straight off the set of *Let's Make a Deal*.

"So what's behind door number one?" She playfully nodded to the one on the right.

"That's the pantry," Brandon replied.

"And how about the one on the left?" she asked.

"That's the second pantry."

"Two pantries?"

"Waste not, want not," Brandon said. "Just like the noble indigenous Tongva Peoples that once inhabited the Los Angeles basin, using every part of the buffalo, or whatever it was they hunted out here. I'm descended from them, ya know. A tribal chief, no less. I am *proudly* 1/32ᵗʰ Tongva. It's even in my Wikipedia bio. This was all our land before the white man came and stole it away."

"Is that a fact?" Déjà said to the blonde-haired blue-eyed man who winked back at her very Anglo-Saxonly. "And the middle door then? What's that? A *third* pantry?"

"Actually, that one leads to the basement. But we don't need to go down there. It's still unfinished. Storage space, really. Come . . . "

They made their way into the spacious living room, where a leather, U-shaped sectional sofa took up the majority of the square footage, facing a large flat-panel TV.

Dolby speakers were placed strategically throughout, just like in the theater. It made Déjà's laptop-in-bed setup at home look laughable by comparison.

Coffee table in the middle with warming coasters for hot drinks, cooling cozies for cold ones. Lights on a dimmer switch, controlled by remote. A thick syringe was left lying out with some kind of clear, gelatinous fluid inside. Words on the side identified what it was, though from where Déjà stood she couldn't make out exactly what it said. Insulin, she figured. Or maybe a workout booster or something. Brandon didn't appear overly concerned about it as he opened a drawer on the side of the table and tucked the needle away.

"That was where I saw you for the very first time." He pointed to the spot on the couch. "Watching the screener of *Leftover Parts*. The studio dropped it off that afternoon, but I didn't get a chance to check it out until dinnertime. Had a glass of Shiraz in one hand and a mustard meat sandwich in the other."

"A mustard meat sandwich?"

"Protein, little darling. Helps me maintain my physique. Orders from Dr. Weldon Fish, Surgeon to the Stars™ and my personal physician. The mustard part is just for flavor. Gives it a bit of a zing," he said. "Anyway, it was only an early cut of the episode. Still a bit rough around the edges. Production was fine. Selena was fine. The whole cast was fine. And then we got to your scene. And I sat up. I said to myself, who is this bewitching woman on my television set right now? I looked you up on IMDb and couldn't believe you had nothing else in pre-production. Such natural grace. Such raw talent. There are a lot of beautiful and brilliant people in this city, but they don't make 'em all like you, Déjà. I've been in this industry a long time. I can sense these kinds of things. You're like this berry just waiting to be plucked. *Juicer* than the rest of 'em. I honestly don't know how else to explain it."

"Oh stop." Déjà let a curly lock of hair fall in front of

her face. She couldn't suppress her smile as she bashfully brushed it aside.

"It's all true," he said. "In fact, Alice? Hey, Alice?"

The maid poked her head into the room. "Yes, Mr. Bowers?"

"Alice, what did I say when Ms. Seawright first popped up on my screen?"

"You said 'who is this bewitching woman on my television set right now?'"

He turned back to Déjà. "See?"

"This is all just so bizarre," she said. "Like I can't believe I'm actually standing here, in your house. I mean, who could've guessed fate was about to bring us together?"

"Fate can be a fickle mistress sometimes. I'm sure I don't have to tell you that. She'll shine her light on some folks just as quickly as she'll turn her back on others. But we're both here now, aren't we? So I suppose we owe her one."

Déjà walked over to a shelf where all the awards he'd won over the years were displayed. A Golden Globe. A BAFTA. One from the Screen Actors Guild. Another from the Florida Film Critics Association. And in the middle— the sun around which all the other awards orbited—a replica of an Oscar, the name BRANDON BOWERS hastily scrawled on the pedestal in permanent black marker. She smirked.

"What's the story here?"

"Oh yeah, that. Ha. Sorta a gag, I suppose." He ran his hand across the back of his neck. "I saw it at a prop shop on Fairfax. Thought maybe I could . . . manifest myself a real one, I guess you could say. Focus that *Oscar energy* into the room. Show the Universe this exact spot on this exact shelf is exactly where this exact award belongs. It's stupid, I know . . . "

"No," Déjà cooed. "I think it's sweet. When I was a little girl, I used to practice making acceptance speeches in the mirror. I'd never been in anything, of course—I hadn't even started acting yet—but in my mind, I was already a star. I even had the list of people I wanted to thank already written. I kept it under my mattress like it was a porno magazine or something."

She picked up the fake award. The gold paint on it was cheap. Peeling off. Revealing the cast of the black statuette underneath. "It's heavy."

"It's made of lead."

"I woulda pegged you as a shoo-in with *Echo Chamber*. Easily your best performance in a decade. Er . . . um . . . not that the others were bad . . ."

"Ha. If only the Academy were so kind. Guess that was just DiCaprio's make-up year, eh? Nah, I joke. He earned it. He earned it." She could hear his teeth grinding. "Always the bridesmaid and never the bride, right?"

"Still got time," she said.

"A lot of people look at me and think, I've made it. I've already won. I'm at the top of the mountain and there's nowhere left to go. Alexander wept, and all that jazz. I see it with my peers sometimes, once they reach a certain level. Kicking their heels back, phoning in their performances, picking easy projects, like life was merely a vacation from here on out. What they don't know is that stagnation is the first step toward entropy. If you stop wanting, you'll start rotting. When you get to the top and you look out at the world, what you should see are *other* challenges, *other* mountains to climb, sprawled out endlessly in every direction. That is the essence of art. That is why I do what I do."

Déjà swooned. She couldn't have said it better herself. In fact, she was reminded of a conversation she had with her mother, almost a year ago now, on the day she left Eau Claire.

"I still don't understand why you have to leave," her mother said as Déjà finished packing her 2004 Honda Civic, the backseat stuffed with whatever she could fit, tossing all the rest of her belongings into the trash. She could buy new stuff when she got to Hollywood, she figured. A whole new life was waiting for her. "You could be an actor right here. You could be an actor anywhere."

"Did they ask Claude Monet to paint houses?"

"What are you talking about?"

"What I'm after doesn't exist in Wisconsin," Déjà said. "It doesn't exist anywhere else in the world except LA. You go where you're called, Mom. That's what a calling is. You of all people should know that."

Her mother fiddled with the tiny gold crucifix she wore around her neck, squeezing the cross between her thumb and index finger, a nervous habit, made all the more dramatic by the bags under her tired eyes and the skunk stripe cutting through the hair on the side of her head. "*For behold, I am sending among you serpents, vipers which cannot be charmed, and they shall bite you, and you shall suffer,*" she said. "*For my grief is beyond healing, and my heart is faint within me.*"

"Really, Mom? Bible quotes? That shit didn't work on me when I was 10, and it's certainly not gonna work on me now."

"I understand you hafta do what you hafta do." Her mother had tears in her eyes. "But you can't change the world without the world changing you as well. One day you might look back and find we've already moved on without you."

"Yeah?" Déjà slammed the truck shut. "Same."

The rift that formed between them that day had never fully closed. It was like they were two different species, speaking in two different tongues. When they talked on the phone, it was brief, distant, compulsory. Now in the living room of Brandon Bowers' massive estate, 1500 miles from where she started, Déjà placed the fake Oscar back down on the mantel and ironically felt closer to God than she'd ever felt before.

ooweeooweeoowoo

The doorbell suddenly rang, shocking Déjà out of her

reverie. Her head snapped in Brandon's direction. "Expecting someone?" she asked.

"Mayyyybeeee . . . " He wiggled his eyebrows at her. "It's a surprise. C'mon."

He took her by the hand and led her back into the entryway. The doorbell rang again. And again. And once more. Each ring coming closer than the one before it, more impatient than the last. Beyond the frosted glass, the outline of two figures stood. Déjà could hear their muffled voices, chattering away.

"Trust me, little darling, you're gonna love this," Brandon said as he swung open the door to reveal Marybelle Ashton and Charlie Eccentric on the other side.

CHAPTER THREE

A DARK TURN

(2008)
DIR. BY BETHANY MARIE CHISHOLM

"... *Bowers' considerable charisma is on full, exploitative display as he shoots and quips his way across this big-budget sci-fi military action extravaganza. Unfortunately, for most of the runtime, it's style over substance, hobbling any of the emotional beats in favor of broad humor and computer-generated spectacle. It's not a bad film exactly, especially on the technical level. It's just vacuous in its delivery. A successful opening weekend all but guarantees a sequel, but it's clear to this reviewer that this is due in no small part to the goodwill Bowers has amassed over the past few years, with* A Dark Turn *serving as a transitional vehicle for the model-turned-indie darling-turned-above-the-title star. As to whether we're witnessing the birth of the next Willis or Schwarzenegger, I guess only time will tell ...*"

DÉJÀ SEAWRIGHT WAS abuzz with anxious energy, trying to play it aloof, play it undaunted, play it confident and cordial and cool.

You're an actress, she said to herself, *so act like you belong here.*

She and Brandon Bowers and Marybelle Ashton and Charlie Eccentric were sitting out on the veranda together like the oldest of friends. That's what this patio thingy was, right? The veranda? Shit, she knew she should've googled it earlier.

The four of them were gathered around a gas-powered lava stone fire pit. Orange flames flickered softly in the breeze. Déjà looked at her shadow, limbs cast long and inhuman across the backyard. Somewhere in the dark, a peacock trilled.

Charlie held a bottle of Dom Pérignon in one hand, a champagne flute in the other which he refilled and drained without reservation. He swayed gently in his seat, thin pale lips curved up at the corners, through which he kept giggling to himself, high-pitched and breathy, as if he were a balloon slowly leaking out air.

Marybelle sat with feet tucked under her on the rattan chaise lounge, looking just as petite as she was in pictures. She had on a slick black dress, similar to the one she wore to the premiere of *Price of Gold*, which was incidentally one of Déjà's favorite movies growing up. She even remembered the synopsis from the back cover of the DVD:

California. The Bay Area. 1849. After the tragic death of her father, a brassy young woman (Marybelle Ashton) vows to save the family farm after gold is discovered in the hills just beyond the property line, enlisting a caddish motormouth (MTV Movie Award-winning actor, Ryan Reynolds) to help.

In true screwball fashion, at first they don't get along,

but by the end of the film they're in love. A ROM-COM CLASSIC!

Big expensive hoops dangled from Marybelle's pierced ears and her eyebrows were a set of perfectly contoured arches. She was pointy-chinned and gumdrop-eyed and flawlessly skinned, though perhaps not quite as flawless as it once was, Déjà noted. Tiny wrinkles besieged all her corners when she smiled, worming their way through the makeup caked onto her face. Although Marybelle's beauty would likely never fade, middle age seemed intent on leaving its mark on her, however subtle it may be.

Brandon reached out and gave Déjà's knee a firm little squeeze, his body language equal parts possessive ("she's mine") and proud ("she's WITH me.") Déjà didn't pull away, but responded in kind, sliding over a few more inches, closing the gap between them on the two-person patio bench. The rhythm of her breath, the flutter of her eyelashes, the heaving of her tiny breasts—a message to everyone here, and anyone else who might be looking on from afar, perhaps the invisible eye of the adoring public that didn't-quite-know she existed yet: You got it backward, my friends. Can't you see? He's *MINE*. *HE'S* with *ME*. I am not the trophy here. *HE* is.

"So that's an interesting jacket," Charlie said to Déjà. "It's very . . . " he waved his hand in the air, conjuring up the word he was looking for " . . . *vintage* . . . " being the one he eventually landed on, though he could barely get it out as he stifled another bout of the titters. Marybelle hit him with her foot. Gave him a stern and admonishing look. Keep it together, her look seemed to say, without having to say anything at all. A real emotive face, Marybelle had, which was perhaps a big factor in why she'd been so successful in the past. She could tell a whole story with her eyes, with just a cock of her head. Almost subconsciously, Déjà tried to mimic her expression, adding it to her oeuvre to pull out at the next audition.

Charlie crossed his legs and leaned back, self-satisfied,

still smirking. He wore a skinny-cut silver suit and matching blazer, with a solid black shirt underneath, punctuated by a slim red tie. His round dark sunglasses never left his head, too cool to take them off, even though it must have been nearly impossible to see in the low porch light.

Charlie was not an actor like the three of them but a pop artist of international renown, in much the same vein as Andy Warhol, whom he clearly modeled his entire image after in a sort of tongue-in-cheek homage. Charlie Eccentric: fashion icon, agent provocateur, and between his celebrity clientele and his own buzz-generating work (the latest of which consisted of a live tadpole crucified in a jar full of his own ejaculate, a piece he entitled KERMIT H. CHRIST), he was the single most recognizable artist working today.

"Huh?" Déjà gave herself a little inspection. She'd forgotten she had the worn-out old jacket on. "Oh. Yeah, thanks."

"It even has that *vintage smell* to it," Charlie added. "You know what I mean, don't you? That *real people* smell."

"One of the only things I brought with me from Eau Claire. A toothbrush and this jacket. Just a little piece of home."

"So a farm girl, are ya?" Charlie finished off another glass of champagne. "A milkmaid, perhaps?"

"Oh my god, Charlie, shut up," Marybelle said. "Eau Claire isn't farmland."

"What the hell is it then?"

"It's like a small city. It's Americana. Apple pie and baseball and white picket fences and all that shit. I shot *Arcadian Rhythm* out there."

"You did?" Déjà asked.

"Yeah," Marybelle replied. Then she thought about it for a second. "Well, actually, no. Not exactly. We mostly shot on a sound stage in Burbank. And the majority of the exteriors were in Petaluma. But the point I'm trying to make is the story took *place* in Eau Claire, so I like to think I know a thing or two about Minnesota."

"Wisconsin," Déjà corrected her.

"What?"

"Eau Claire is in Wisconsin."

"You sure?"

"Yeah, I'm sure."

"Huh. Guess I was just too busy getting into character to worry about the topography of the thing. I played Melody Marx, a disgraced pop singer forced to hide out back in her hometown after a tabloid scandal threatened to derail her career. Of course, coming back home to reconcile with her past has some unintended consequences, not the least of which is the rekindling of the romance with her old high school sweetheart, Chet Stanton. Her entire value system is uprooted in the process, and by the end of the movie, she learns about what's *truly* important in life. I did all my own singing for that role, if you recall. Got vocal lessons from Lis Lewis. She's worked with some of the best. Rihanna. Gwen Stefani. Britney Spears, back in the day."

"Yes yes, we ALL remember *Arcadian Rhythm* . . . " Brandon rolled his eyes. He turned toward Déjà. "One of the biggest returns of her career, and she never lets us forget it."

"We were at nearly a 10x multiplier the month after release!" Marybelle said. "That's nothing to balk at!"

"See?" Brandon replied, arms outstretched, as if she'd proven his point for him.

"Oh please," she brushed him off. "Like you ever shut up about missing *Iron Man*. You're like a broken record."

"I was *this* close! I even screen tested!"

"And I was *this* close to getting the Jennifer Lawrence part in *Silver Linings Playbook* too, but you don't hear me whining about it a decade later," Marybelle said. "It's just the nature of the beast. You know that as well as I do, Brandon. We're all vying for a piece of the pie. You have no idea how many times I prayed for Reese Witherspoon to get into a car accident, or for a loose brick to fall on Sandy Bullock's head. I mean, shit dude, I could fill a book with all the great roles I was considered for and didn't get."

"*I Could Do Your Job Better Than You: Sour Grapes and Other Gripes,* a New York Times Bestseller, by Marybelle Ashton," Charlie suggested as a title.

"Very funny," Marybelle bemusedly replied. "It's not like I see you doing more than picture books yourself, Mr. Edgy Artist. *Photographs of My Used Toilet Paper and Other Lazy Works of Transgression* by Fading International Firebrand, Charlie Eccentric."

"Ouf. Claws are comin' out tonight, aren't they?"

"Hey, I'm calling it like I see it."

Charlie rolled his eyes. "Listen, honey. I bet I could write the Great American Novel if I wanted to, but both fiction and non-fiction alike, it's all just so *pedestrian.* Who's even got the time to read a book these days, let alone write one? That's why I have decided to *transcend* the written word and make statements more powerful and evocative than any book could ever contain. Far as I'm concerned KERMIT H. CHRIST says everything that needs to be said about the human condition. It's basically my *War and Peace.*"

Brandon cleared his throat. "All I can tell you for certain is that every time I run into Downey Jr., I never let that little twerp live it down. $430 million. That's how much he's made over the years for playing Iron Man. $430 MILLION! 'Shoulda been me,' I say to him. 'I shoulda been Marvel's poster boy.' I mean, look at me. I'm cut like the Charles Atlas. Did you know Downey's only 5'9"? Dude shoulda played Ant Man."

"Now *THOSE* are some sour grapes," Charlie said.

"You know what I think?" Déjà chimed in a little too vociferously, trying to match the mounting energy of everyone else and overshooting the mark. All three of them turned to her, as if she'd just reminded them she was there.

"No, what do you think, little darling?" There was the slightest hint of condescension in Brandon's tone, this country mouse of a girl at his side, suddenly so full of opinions.

Déjà was pretty sure she had a bit too much to drink. But too late now. She was already talking. "I think y'all are living the kinds of lives most normal people could only dream of. And I think you've all been at it so long, you've lost sight of how lucky you are. You're out here, achieving your dreams every goddamn day, doing the kind of good work that'll all but ensure you'll be revered and remembered for generations to come. That is so much more than I can say for anybody I knew back home."

"Here we go," Marybelle snorted. "This old chestnut. 'Count your blessings. You don't know how good you have it' Blah blah blah blah. Look lady, whoever you are, just because we got it easy doesn't mean we got it *easy*, okay?"

But Déjà was determined to finish her thought. "I'm just saying, maybe you all would feel a lot more fulfilled if you stopped concentrating on the things you *haven't* accomplished and started focusing on the things you *have*. The lives you touched. The legacies you'll leave behind. I guess my point is, you don't necessarily need to be Iron Man to be a hero."

"Well would'ja listen to her." Charlie gulped down another flute of champagne. "Where did you find this one, Brandon? Like a babe in the woods. 'The lives you touched?' How maudlin can you get? Honestly, for a second there, I thought she was gonna start quoting from *Eggs with a Side of Hope* at us . . . "

"Oh god!" an exasperated Marybelle Ashton exclaimed. "You just *had* to go there, didn't you?"

"What? That *was* a movie you and Brandon were both in, was it not? I'm not telling tales outta school, now am I? I mean, we could check IMDb, just to make sure . . . "

"Yeah, Charlie. We were both in it." Brandon pinched

the bridge of his nose with his thumb and index finger. "But as I've told you 100 times before, we don't talk about *Eggs* in this house. You KNOW we don't talk about *Eggs* in this house."

"Am I missing something?" asked Déjà. "What's wrong with *Eggs with a Side of Hope*?"

"I think the more pressing question would be, what's *right* with it?" Charlie said.

"You have seen the film, haven't you?" Brandon asked her.

"Well, yeah." Déjà's eyes flicked to the left and the right, as if the movie were replaying itself inside her head. "I mean, it wasn't *that* bad . . . "

This elicited a round of uproarious laughter from the whole party. Brandon included.

Marybelle wiped away a tear. "Oh that's rich."

"Honey, you don't hafta do that," Charlie said.

Déjà was genuinely confused by their reaction. She wasn't trying to be funny. "Don't hafta do what?"

"You don't hafta pretend you liked that stinker of a film. You got no reason to kiss Brandon's hairy ass anymore. You're already in the house."

"It has its moments." She turned to Brandon and Marybelle. "You were both . . . *charming* in it . . . "

Brandon took her hands into his. "Listen Déjà, I appreciate the fluff job, but if you keep on insisting that you liked that piece of crap, I might have to start questioning your sanity. Or, at the very least, your taste."

"And keep in mind, this is coming from the guy who starred in that ridiculous *Mr. Ed* reboot like six months later," Marybelle added.

"Oh my god." Brandon ran a hand through his hair. "That fucking horse would NOT stop shitting all over the set . . . "

Once again, everyone laughed, and this time, Déjà joined in.

"And on that note, a toast!" Charlie raised his glass. "To

Mr. Ed and all the other workhorses in the industry. For they are the glue that holds this whole town together."

The rest of them toasted Charlie back.

"To Mr. Ed," they all said in unison.

And the night continued on, as nights like this often did, full of rambling and effortless conversation, good-natured ribbing, and open and affable cheer. And perhaps it was the three glasses of wine working their way through her bloodstream, but Déjà Seawright, who had only been in Los Angeles for less than a year, found herself growing exceedingly comfortable in her extravagant surroundings and with her famous company. Her mother had sounded an alarm that clearly needn't be rung. Who were these so-called snakes? And why on Earth would they be trying to bite *her*? Though these people weren't her friends yesterday, she certainly felt like she might be able to call them such tomorrow.

Alice approached, carrying the same silver platter Déjà put her shoes and her phone on earlier. She placed the tray on the table next to the fire pit and pulled off the lid. Déjà was expecting some snacks or something. Crudités or a charcuterie plate. At least some cheese and crackers. It'd been hours since she'd eaten.

But instead of food, on the platter was a pile of shiny purple-gray powder stacked about an inch high, along with four short straws, one for each of them.

"Finally!" Charlie didn't even bother to cut a rail as he leaned over, grabbed the tube, and from the center of the pile, sucked a fat bump of the substance up through his nose. He leaned back, grunting, grinding, muscles flexing, stringy tendons like harp strings on his straining neck. "Fuuuuuck," he bellowed as Marybelle grabbed a straw and took a bump too.

For her part, Marybelle was more composed than the

flamboyant artist, though Déjà could tell that by the flare of her nostrils and quickening of her breath that she too was experiencing some kind of rush.

Déjà turned to Brandon. "Is that . . . cocaine?"

"Oh please," Marybelle answered for him with a dismissive wave of the hand. "I don't even put sugar in my coffee. It ain't the 80s anymore, child. Modern times call for modern solutions."

"So it's not coke?"

"What are we, in grade school?" Charlie spoke through his clenched teeth. "You gonna make sure I've eaten all my veggies too?"

"No, it's not coke." Brandon picked up a straw and snorted some of the powder up his nose as well. He squeezed his fists tight. Cracked his knuckles. In his lap, Déjà could again see his stumpy yet inexhaustible erection pressing taut against his slacks.

"That's a hard pass for me when it comes to the devil's dust, thankyouverymuch," Marybelle said. "Haven't touched the stuff since my 20s. It's terrible for the skin, ya know. We're trying to fight the wrinkles over here, not give 'em a leg up."

"Plus I've done coke with her, and it ain't pretty," Charlie said. "Swear to god, I saw her eat a live rat once."

"Shut up. I did not."

"Rat. Squirrel. Whatever it was. I'm not a fuckin' rodent scientist."

"So what is it then?" asked Déjà. "Bath salts? PCP?"

Brandon took a few deep breaths, pulling in air and pushing it back out, pupils mere pinpricks in the ocean of his eyes. But still, his voice remained collected and calm, immediately putting her at ease in the same way it had always done from the big screen. "No, no, no. Nothing like that. This is more like . . . um . . . a *vitamin*, I guess you could say. Naturally sourced, of course. We're talking high-grade stuff, though it's not exactly easy to come by, which is why we only break it out on special occasions. Nights like tonight."

"What does it do?"

"What *doesn't* it do, would be a better question. Euphoria. Clarity. Physical and mental strength. It's like eating a slice of your own birthday cake. It's like being born again, better than before. It gives you both a sense of purpose and the road map to get there. It sharpens the senses and really gets the blood pumping."

"We call it Reno," Charlie added.

"Reno, like the city?" asked Déjà.

"Yeah, something like that." Brandon handed his straw off to her. "Toot-toot goes the trolley as it leaves the station."

Déjà looked at the powder again, apprehensive—and, if she were being totally honest with herself, a little afraid. She was no prude. But she wasn't in the habit of doing strange new drugs either. The eager eyes of her new acquaintances were all peeled to her, though. The spotlight fell upon her, Déjà on the center stage.

"Not quite in Kansas anymore, are ya Dorothy?" The smile Charlie Eccentric wore was so wide it looked like his head was going to split in two.

Déjà froze. Glared at the pop artist across from her, his eyes still hidden behind his dark glasses, unknowable. "What did you call me?"

Marybelle bared her teeth, a perfect row of piano keys, her laughter like the accompanying aria. She nudged Charlie with her elbow. "Uh-oh. Looks like you mighta pressed the wrong button there, Chuck . . . "

"Where did you hear that name?" Déjà wanted to shout but she knew better. Still, the tremble in her voice was unmistakable, unavoidable, and only caused Charlie and Marybelle to devolve into further hysterics.

"Oh god, I'm such a bitch, aren't I?" Charlie said. "Was that too bitchy of me? I'm sorry, *Déjà*. DéjàDéjàDéjà. Don'tchu worry, Dorothy Smalls, your secret identity is safe with me. I'm like the Alfred to your Batman. Nothing said here shall ever leave this cave."

STARLET

Déjà's heart was pounding in her chest. *Thump. Thump. Thump.* Echoing like a timpani drum in the back of her ears. The change in the air was almost palpable. Things were suddenly not quite as congenial as they were but a moment before. Emotions swept through her in a brackish mix, joy quickly gave way to confusion, happiness was instantly replaced by distrust. She wasn't Dorothy Smalls anymore, she reminded herself. She hadn't been Dorothy Smalls since she moved to LA. How could Charlie Eccentric have possibly known her real name?

She needed Brandon. She needed her big, strong leading man to put his friends in their place. She turned to her right, but before she knew what was happening, Brandon pinched up a handful of the purple powder and blew it at her. *Poof.* The sparkling dust surrounded her in a cloud from which she could not escape.

"What the fuck!" Déjà coughed and hacked and wheezed as the mysterious substance entered her airway. Her nose and mouth and esophagus burned like the house were burning down around her. The Reno filled her skull and dripped down the back of her throat.

Brandon took Déjà's hands into his and pulled her close. "Shhhh. There, there. No need to fret, little darling. Like I said, it's naturally sourced. Everything you're feeling is perfectly natural. Dr. Fish says it's supposed to sting a bit. That just means it's working."

The drug set the tempo, her heart was a punk rock show, a mosh pit of sensations that threatened to claw her apart from the inside out. She had no choice but to give into the melee. To become one with the chaos inside her as the Reno took hold.

And for the briefest of moments, Déjà found the euphoria Brandon had promised, unburdened and full and content and free. What had once been a hidden light now shined upon her from within. She saw the shape of her own soul and was awed by the splendor it was able to contain. It was like God Himself parted the seas and the earth and the skies to baptize her with His holy and unimpeachable decree: *You are special, Déjà Seawright. You are better than everyone else. You were born to feel this way. And you deserve all the love and good fortune that will one day betide you.*

"Oh man, our girl is HIIIIIGH." Charlie stuck his straw back into the grainy pyramid and snorted another noseful. Marybelle and Brandon did the same. Toot. Toot. Toot. The three of them kept their collective gaze peeled toward Déjà, swaying gently in her seat. "And if I'm reading her face correctly, she should be coming around the bend right . . . about . . . now . . . "

And almost as suddenly as it arrived, the light inside her faded away. The God who just promised her the world returned to His silent throne. The rollercoaster she was on reached its inevitable apogee, and on the other side of the drop, there was only fear.

"What is happening to me?" Déjà could barely talk. Barely move. Her limbs transformed into a cluster of cargo ship anchors. It took all her strength just to keep breathing, to keep sitting up.

Charlie was giggling like a hyena. Charlie never stopped giggling. Even when he was talking, even when he pressed his lips shut, he seemed to still be giggling somehow, as if the laughter were coming not just from his mouth, but from his nose and his ears and his eyes as well, high-pitched and vicious and humming out of his pores.

The three celebrities circled Déjà like a school of sharks around a puddle of chum.

"Look at the size of those pupils!" Charlie Eccentric held open her left eyelid to show Brandon and Marybelle. "Now THAT is what I call mortal terror! I can smell that adrenal gland plumping up from here. This is going to be a good night indeed."

Brandon pressed his nose to her neck and inhaled. He moved to her armpits. Her clavicle. Her crotch. A bloodhound locking onto her scent. The erection in his pants once more sprung to life and another ovular jism stain appeared on the front of his chinos. He rolled off her. Lit a post-coital cigarette. Took a dramatic draw. Curls of smoke rose from the cherry end as cum continued to fill his trousers, an orgasm that refused to end, soaking into the cushion beneath him. "Yes, this *berry* is getting *juicy* indeed."

Marybelle *tsk-tsk*ed Brandon, sitting unapologetic in his salty sticky mess. She remained more poised than her boorish male counterparts. Back in 2006 she was voted one of the Most Influential Women of the New Millennium in an online poll by *People Magazine.* With her perfectly-coiffed hair and perfectly-fitted clothes tailored to fit her perfectly-proportional 5'3" frame, even now, nearly two decades later and high as a kite on this Reno shit, she still looked like she just stepped right out of the pages of that stately publication.

"Poor little Dorothy. Or should I say Déjà. Or whoever the fuck it is you think you are. Open your eyes, you silly child. You think beauty is rare? Especially in this town? Especially in this business? Take a gander at those peacocks out there. They're beautiful, alright, but at the end of the day, they're just birds, and they look the same. And the same goes for talent too. We're surrounded by talent. We're drowning in talent. Girls like you flow through this city like the river after the rain. This is a well that will never run dry. The Aspiring Actress. The Plucky Young Starlet. I mean, really Déjà, could you be any more of a cliche?"

Overhead, a passenger plane hummed across the clear, dark sky. A tiny dot of light, 30,000 feet away.

"There is this concept in arts called *verisimilitude*. Are you familiar with the term, Dorothy Smalls?" Déjà felt like her mouth was packed with steel wool. No space for words. No space to scream. Not that it would've made a difference anyway. Marybelle wasn't interested in anything Déjà had to say. This was her monologue. And it sounded like a well-rehearsed one at that. "When you go to the movies, you know the things portrayed on the screen aren't real. And yet, if the movie is any good at least, it should be able to break through the artifice anyway. It should elicit emotion. It should thrill. It should resonate. It should affect. *Verisimilitude* is the appearance of truth at the heart of the lie. It's that which allows you to suspend your disbelief. It's the moment when you and the artifice become one . . . "

Marybelle dipped the pad of her finger into her eye and pulled out a contact lens. Then she did the other. Her famously cerulean irises were now the color of coal, two sunken black lumps smoldering in her face.

"Stupid contacts are always drying out," she said before reaching up and grabbing her hair on either side of her temples and sliding it off. A blonde wig. She tossed it on the table, next to the Reno. She ran her hands across her bald, misshapen head—clumps of thin, pube-like hair grew in patches between the swollen blue veins traversing her skull. "Sometimes it feels good to just let your hair down, ya know?"

"What . . . the . . . fuck . . . ?" The words spilled out of Déjà like vomit, the first words she was able to articulate in the past 10 minutes, and perhaps the only appropriate response to terror unfolding before her.

Marybelle Ashton peeled apart her makeup, from the top of her forehead to the bottom of her chin, like her face was sloughing off in one big sheet. Her skin was blemished, brown-spotted, wrinkled, cadaverous. No longer the person she was a few minutes ago, Marybelle now stood before Déjà, unadorned, inhuman.

Charlie took another snort of Reno and snatched Marybelle's wig off the table. He stuck it haphazardly on his head. "*Have I ever told you about how many dicks I had to suck to score the lead in* Arcadian Rhythm?" he said in a mock falsetto. "*Ten thousand dicks, each one more wart-covered than the last!*"

"Cut it out." Marybelle shoved him and Charlie

bumped into the chaise. He managed to catch himself from falling, but in the process, his sunglasses slipped off his head. In place of his eyes were two extra sets of mouths. They were not quite as fully formed as his normal mouth, and the teeth inside them were small and rotten, like tiny kernels of greasy corn, but they seemed to work the way mouths were supposed to. Tongues darted in and out. Drool ran down the bridge of his nose like tears. All three of them were giggling, giggling, and giggling some more.

Brain still spinning, body still numb, Déjà braced herself and focused as much energy as she could into her legs, pushing through the mental molasses. Like a toddler she rose to her feet and stumbled back a step. Jell-O knees. "Brandon . . ." Her desperate eyes turned to the marquee star she spent the last month flirting with online. ". . . help . . ."

Brandon shook his head. No can do, little darling. Sorry, not sorry. And he began to transform too. His eyebrows dislodged themselves from his forehead, were left adrift on his countenance until they settled on opposite sides of his face like muttonchops. His hairline receded. His jowls dropped. He reached into his mouth and removed his dentures. Brandon Bowers dismantled himself in front of her, a haggard old man shedding his skin.

"Contrary to what Marybelle might say, I don't think you're disposable at all," he said. "That was why I was drawn to you in the first place. I know it might seem like little consolation now, but you actually do have something special, Déjà. That indefinable quality that draws people in. The 'it' factor, as they say. That certain *je ne sais quoi*."

He unbuttoned his shirt and revealed the corset he wore underneath. It was drawn tight, shaping his torso, tucking certain parts in, moving other parts around.

He pulled on a string and the girdle burst open like a dam buckling under the weight of floodwaters. A big chubby belly spilled out of his front and a large

DANGER SLATER

Quasimodo-like hump popped up on his back. His posture buckled. He looked like an overinflated letter C.

"I don't wear the girdle all the time," Brandon said. "Just at the end of the cycle, when things start . . . slipping out of place. It's just so hard to keep up appearances sometimes. Even a star of my caliber has to take every advantage I can get. I mean, I don't even have my Oscar yet, Déjà. It's no time to rest on my laurels. You gotta understand where I'm coming from, right?"

Déjà backed into Alice who had crept up behind her to block the exit. The maid stared unblinkingly ahead. Dead-eyed. Tight-lipped. An immovable object. Forever the loyal servant.

Déjà knew that her pleas would only fall on deaf ears. But she pleaded with them anyway because what else could she do? "I'll do anything you want, just please let me go."

The three celebrities closed in. Charlie scooped up another palmful of Reno. *Poof.* All three of his mouths blew in unison. The powder billowed out, a cloud so big it enveloped all of them in an instant. Purple granules twinkled like stars in the sky. Déjà felt like her blood was made of napalm. Fear, as unbridled and intense as she'd ever known, charged through her. And when Brandon spoke to her, his once familiar voice now sounded infinitely more sinister, as her consciousness flickered. Fizzled. Short circuited. And cut out.

"C'mon, Dorothy. Click your heels together and say it with me now. I know you know the line. *There's no place like home. There's no place like home. There's no place like home. There's no place like home . . .*"

CHAPTER FOUR

BODY OF WORK

(2009)
DIR. BY HANNIBAL HOOPER

" . . . the problem with Body of Work is not so much the script, which is serviceable, nor is it Hooper's direction, uninspired it may be. The problem is that while Brandon Bowers certainly exudes plenty of confidence onscreen as the art-curator-turned-amateur-detective Polestar Ganz, he isn't bringing anything new to the part we haven't seen from him before. There is a kind of complacency to his performance—a been-there-done-that sort of savoir-faire that seems inherent to Bowers himself and is at odds with the haunting intensity this kind of character demands. The result is, of course, a somewhat lackluster and wildly uneven film that never quite satisfies on any level . . . "

THE SOUND OF CLANKING. Metal against metal. Things being shuffled around her. A breath so hot and heavy and close it stuck to her skin like the gas from a swamp.

When she was a young girl, Déjà had a friend whose father ran the local funeral parlor, which he operated out of the basement of their two-story home. Bodies flowed through the parlor, day and night, death not beholden to office hours or scheduled appointments—an endless procession of unmarked minivans, hauling corpses in to be prepared, and hauling them back out again for their services and memorials. Déjà never went down there, into the basement, into the embalming room, even when her friend implored her to, even when she called her a chicken. *C'mon, ya big baby, don'tcha wanna see a dead body?* her friend would tease. *It's not like it's gonna jump up off the table and bite you.* And Young Déjà would make a disgusted face and shake her head no. *Sorry, but I ain't interested in your creep show, friendo.* And the two of them would laugh and run off to go do something else.

But that was only half the story. Because it didn't really matter if they went into the basement or not. Because death was determined to come find them instead. And the stench of bodies in various stages of decay would waft up through the air vents and fill the rest of the house like a ghost. Seeping into the floorboard. Impregnating the walls. Even in the backyard they couldn't quite escape it, an indescribable and horrid bouquet, somehow both chemical and biological, pickled and sharp. Perhaps her friend was used to it. But Déjà was not.

Even all these years later, the memory of it still lingered. It was the exact same stench that permeated the room in which Déjà now blinked herself awake.

Above her, a surgical lamp bombarded the scene with 300 watts of shadowless light. Bright. Sterile. White. And for a moment, she thought that maybe she'd been abducted by aliens. This was how they always depicted alien abductions in the movies. A large empty luminous void. The abductee strapped to a table, such as she was, wires running from her body to a piece of inexplicable machinery, the monitors surrounding her glowing green. A series of beeps and blips quickened along with her heart rate, some kind of EKG-type thing feeding data into a computer set up on a cart nearby.

She attempted to raise her arm but it was belted down to the table along with the rest of her limbs. There was no sitting up. No running away.

Beside her was a tray with a bunch of tools out on it. Scoopers and scalpels, prongs and tines, an odd combination of rusty steel cutlery. And what was the one on the end, bigger and sharper than the rest? Was that a *bone saw*?! Oh god.

Clomp. Clomp. Clomp.

Oxford heels tapped the tile. Déjà had no idea from which direction they came or went. Her brain felt waterlogged. Her thoughts moved as if she were trapped in a dream. The Reno still surged through her, blossoming into a paradox of sensations, somehow dull yet overwhelming. The only emotion she could get a foothold on was fear.

"Oh good, you're awake."

The voice that spoke to her was unfamiliar, masculine yet soft, and sprinkled with a sibilant sort of lilt. It was the kind of voice built for telling bedtime stories, soothing and soporific. And it did not belong to Brandon Bowers or Charlie Eccentric or anyone she had met so far.

"Who are you? Who's there?" Déjà was in no position to make demands. But the voice complied anyway. A man in his late 60s leaned over and waved hello.

"The name is Fish," he said. "Dr. Weldon Fish: Surgeon to the Stars™. Perhaps you've seen the ads on Rodeo or heard our jingle on the radio? ♪ *when you need a new nose or a few extra toes, call Dr. Fish and he'll get you some of those ♪"* His pale, dehydrated lips were pinched upward and pinned back, leaving a permanent smile on his plastic-looking face, and his skin was unnaturally shiny and smooth, as if it had been sandblasted free of wrinkles. Thin eyebrows appeared as if they were tattooed on and his nose was little more than two slits sitting just above his mouth. He looked like a poorly rendered version of a human being, like from an old video game, 16-bits deep into the uncanny valley. "No? Well, it's been a few years since we last ran those commercials. Maybe you're a bit too young."

He picked up his scalpel. Tested the sharpness by touching it lightly to his thumb. A little drop of blood bubbled out, so red it looked like paint. He put it in his mouth. Sucked until it ran dry.

"I actually don't do much surgery these days. No need. I've moved on to a more exclusive patronage and more lucrative endeavors. Of course, I guess you could *technically* call what I'm about to do to you surgery, but I'd say it's more akin to playing the pipe organ than a medical procedure. More art than science, is what I'm saying. I'm like Bach or Mozart or one of those guys."

She was in some kind of operating suite, an eight-foot pit encircled by a mezzanine, like a theater in the round. Three dark figures watched from above, as if she and this mad doctor were about to perform *As You Like It* for them. *All the world is a stage, and all the men and women are merely players . . .*

"What the fuck is happening, you fucking asshole?" Déjà shouted, perhaps not quite as eloquent as Shakespeare would've put it, but sufficiently dramatic, nonetheless. She thrashed, but her bindings held tight. "Where am I? What the hell is this?"

"Whoa, whoa, whoa. Roll it back. One question at a time, please."

"Untie me."

"That wasn't a question."

"You hanging in there, little darling?" From the balcony, Brandon leaned forward so that she could make out his face through the fog of light. His features had returned to their rightful places since she'd last seen him. Eyebrows atop his forehead. Hunchback refolded in. Next to him, Charlie was wearing his sunglasses and Marybelle had reattached her wig. The three of them were back to their normal, camera-ready selves.

"You've just had a bit too much to drink is all," said the doctor.

"Too much to drink?" Déjà repeated in disbelief.

"Yup. Passed out and hit your head. Tell me, how many fingers am I holding up?" He gave her the middle finger. Déjà screamed for help. Dr. Fish nodded. "Alright, well it seems you've got a handle on yourself, but still, things might appear a little strange or distorted for a bit. Cognitive abilities may be impaired. Motor functions might not be firing at 100%. This is all to be expected, all perfectly normal."

"Perfectly normal for *what*?"

Dr. Fish tweaked the settings on his instruments, checked the readouts on his screens. "I know this is probably not how you imagined this night would turn out, Ms. Seawright, but I want to ensure you that like all good doctors, I abide by the Hippocratic Oath. I am not cruel without necessity. But if you want to make an omelet, you gotta crack a few eggs. This night? These machines? The things I'm about to do to you? Each step has been an integral part of the process. And this is perhaps the most integral part of all. I like to call this part *the marinade*. When you really start stewing in your own juices. That crack of doom. Those unbridled pheromones. Mmmhmm. Sweet ambrosia. I can almost taste you from here."

Dr. Fish readjusted a couple of the wires. The beeps and blips beeped and blipped even faster. "Did you know there is not a part of the body that fear doesn't affect?" he continued. "It's true. Physiologically, psychologically, even spiritually, if you adhere to such things—we all answer to that little light inside ourselves, the one that never stops flicking until the day it goes out. *Danger*, it might tell us in a moment of panic. *Run away. Fight back. Do whatever you must to SURVIVE*. Fear is perhaps the most base and most powerful of all the emotions, consciously and subconsciously governing all we do, as unavoidable as our breath itself.

"But being afraid all the time is no way to live, now is it? And how is one supposed to go on when the shadow of death engulfs every mortal thing? As I'm sure you could surmise from the array of complicated equipment lain out before you that I am a brilliant and uncommon man, Ms. Seawright, and I spent years asking myself these very deep questions. I thought, what if there was a way to harness that innate sense of fear and make it work *for* us rather than *against* us? What if we could use fear as the catalyst for something much greater, something much more productive?"

Déjà could hardly think straight. The buzz of the machinery. The hoots and hollers from the celebrities above. This plastic-looking doctor and his cryptic little speech. None of it made any goddamn sense.

"That answer, it turned out, was sitting right here the whole time." Dr. Fish tapped Déjà's exposed stomach like he was checking the ripeness of a cantaloupe. "Gathering just beneath the surface of your skin. Because gone are the days of the barbaric nip/tuck. We've been merely filling in potholes when we needed to repave the whole road. We have better methods now. Less invasive methods. Permanent methods. A few shots of DohrniiTox and a surplus of Reno. That's all it takes. One is the lock, and the other is the key, and with the proper regimen, one can stay viable for a long, long time."

"I don't understand," Déjà said. "What is DohrniiTox? What the fuck is Reno???"

"*Adrenochrome* is the scientific term for it." He picked up the bone saw, already glazed in a sheen of bright red blood, and licked it, from the handle to the tip, leaving a slimy tongue mark across the metal. "The chemical byproduct of an overstimulated adrenal gland. One of the most potent compounds that the human body can produce. Think of it like the Special Sauce on a Big Mac, if you will. Or the mythical water they use to make the pizza at Joe Peeps. Do you feel your heart pumping? That flight-or-flight mechanism going off in the most instinctual parts of your brain? That's the adrenaline flooding your system. The adrenochrome in your veins. The gravy. The fertilizer from which the lushest gardens grow."

A sizzle could be heard nearby and a thin trail of smoke hung in the air, carrying with it a smell so savory and delicious and familiar that it made Déjà's mouth water. It reminded her of the barbecues they'd have in the backyard when she was a little girl, where everyone she knew would be in attendance: Her mother's church group. Her meemaw. Her uncles and aunties. The entire neighborhood—a couple dozen people, perhaps more—gathered to enjoy each other's company and have a good time. Déjà would spend the day laughing and playing and running around with her cousins, stopping every once in a while to eat a forkful of macaroni salad or take a bite of a spare rib. *I'mma be a famous actress one day*, she would tell them, even back then. *I'mma be the star of the show*. And her cousins would chime in like parrots. *Me too. Me too. I'mma be famous too*. Everybody wants it, thought Déjà, but she had been the only one with enough fortitude to leave them all behind and truly follow through.

Her eyes darted up to the observation deck, where Brandon, Marybelle, and Charlie were cooking some kind of meat on a portable, kerosene-powered grill.

"Ooooh I think she might be hungry, Charlie," Marybelle said.

"I think you might be right, Marybelle," the pop artist

concurred. Through the haze, Déjà could see him, blood smeared around his lips like clown makeup, chunks of flesh stuck between his teeth. "I really gotta HAND it to you, Déjà. You are quite the SNACK."

The laughter of the three celebrities echoed throughout the room, like the studio audience on some kind of corny sitcom set.

Déjà once again felt her heart begin to hammer as her eyes slowly drifted back down.

Her left hand was missing.

Chopped off and cauterized at the wrist. Dollops of yellow pus seeped out of the spaces between the blistered ribbons of her remaining flesh.

Déjà screamed. Flailed. Tried to kick loose but was unable to move her legs. The machine next to her made all kinds of furious noises and the monitor next to it flashed like lightning as charts and readouts raced across the screen. It was an apocalyptic display. Robots run amok.

Dr. Fish slid over to the computer stand and pecked out a few commands on the keyboard, delighted by what he saw.

"Yes! Yes! Very nice! Very good! Let's keep it going! Let's keep that adrenaline flowing! Fight-or-flight, baby! Fight-or-flight!"

"Let me out of here!" Déjà pushed so hard against her restraints she could not breathe. The straps didn't budge in the slightest.

And the celebrities in the mezzanine were in full-on hysterics. Every time Déjà let out another whimper, the three of them reacted like it was the funniest joke they ever heard.

Charlie took a pair of tongs and picked Déjà's amputated hand off the grill. The skin on it had blackened and blistered, her former fingers bent into a useless claw. He playfully dangled the hand over Marybelle's head, saying, "Who'sa good girl? Who'sa good girl?" over and over again while the star of *Price of Gold* barked like a dog and took little bites out of it. Brandon sat to the right of them, violently bobbing up and down, a determined and pained look on his face as he masturbated himself like a madman, blasting a fresh cumshot at his two friends every 10 seconds or so. Another spasmodic jerk. *Ping*. And another. And another. And another. *Ping. Ping. Ping.* Ropes of jism draped his confidants like tinsel on a Christmas tree.

"Perfect!" Dr. Fish called out to them as he hit the ENTER button with an animated flourish. "You three are like a Renaissance painting. Keep it up."

The table Déjà was strapped to started to move on its own. Gears grinding. Machinery in motion. It rose up and pitched forward, and for a brief moment, she had a good view of the macabre picnic on the balcony, the grill and the bottles of wine and the lounging celebrities. Charlie used her own severed hand to wave to her.

And the table continued along its path, so that Déjà was now suspended upside down, facing the floor. Dr. Fish worked underneath her like she was a Prius on the rack at the mechanics. Just a few inches between her heaving chest and the top of his head.

He wheeled another machine over. A strange, rusty-looking thing, about the size of a hot dog cart, with tubes and nozzles and thick braids of wire coming out of its sides like tentacles. It looked like one of those janky pneumatic air pump things you'd see old-fashioned diving suits attached to. The kind with the big, round copper bell helmets.

Dr. Fish flipped a few levers. The apparatus honked to life. "I just wanted to tell you, Ms. Seawright, that I thought you were really great in that *Leftover Parts* pilot. Brandon showed me the screener during our last DohrniiTox session. Just phenomenal. The vulnerability you brought to . . . what was the character's name again? Matilda Speck? I could tell it was coming from a personal place. That's the thing that separates a true artist from the rest of the rabble, how you are able to internalize and project these dark and often universal truths. Very powerful stuff."

He picked up a large, hollow needle and attached it to one of the clear tubes looping around his feet like a garden hose. An umbilicus plugged into the wheezing device. He tested the suction. Pressed his finger to the hole. Nodded in approval.

"I know it looks complicated, but it's really just a big vacuum cleaner," he said. "The trick is not in the construction, but in the execution. Finding the source. And tapping in."

He lifted her shirt. Felt along her soft and quivering belly, able to intuit what was where underneath. Fingertips traveling to the side, almost around to her back.

"The adrenal glands are located on the top of each kidney. A little white mass, no bigger than a quarter. So much punch in such a small package. Sorta like you. God really has a sick sense of humor like that." The machine thrummed louder. The instrument in his hand made a slurping sound. Dr. Fish had to yell to be heard over it. "As your doctor, I suppose I should warn you that the extraction process is also a fatal one. But no worries, it should only take an hour. Two at the max. So I guess it's time to take your final bow, Ms. Seawright, because here come the curtains."

And he jammed the needle into her abdomen.

Like a gunshot. It hurt. Bad. Déjà ground her teeth so tightly they felt like they were about to shatter.

Dr. Fish hummed blithely to himself as he worked underneath her. The machine next to him guzzled and gulped, a mechanical mosquito, feeding on her adrenal glands, bit by bit. A thick purple substance rippled through the tube-like tree sap and collected into a large bucket at the bottom of the device. 100% pure human sludge. Reno in its most concentrated and unadulterated form.

"It ain't gonna get any fresher than this," Dr. Fish called out to the celebrities on the observation deck. "Come and have a quick sip before these udders run dry."

She could hear their feet thumping down an out-of-sight staircase and into the operating room—Charlie Eccentric, and Marybelle Ashton, and Brandon Bowers, the effortlessly charming A-list actor, who had effortlessly charmed her into this nightmare scenario. All it took was a few flirty messages and the promise of potentially padding her career. How fucking naive could she have been?

"My hand . . . " Déjà's eyes made their way toward the severed appendage, still in Charlie's possession, now just a jangle of blackened bones. Like vultures they had picked the whole thing clean. " . . . you ate it!"

Charlie carelessly tossed it aside like it were nothing more than a watermelon rind. "Puh-leaze, it was like two bites total. Get over yourself."

Déjà tried to stop herself from screaming, tried her best to fight the fear continuously rising inside of her, but as her heart rate increased, so too did the Reno oozing out. The more they terrorized her, the stronger the Reno became. She struggled and squirmed against her bindings, hoping—*praying*—for a weak buckle, for any kind of leverage, finding none beyond the tiniest bit of purchase on the left side, where the strap around her handless wrist tapered off to nothing at the end.

Déjà bent her elbow and hitched and was met with overwhelming resistance. The harness was too tight to pull out of. The pain was too great to endure. More globs of pus were squeezed out of her like lemon curd from the cauterized end. She made slight progress but not enough to break free.

Dr. Fish used the tap on the side of the adrenochrome container to fill three little Dixie cups with the purple goop. He handed them off to his celebrity clientele. They each threw back their heads and tossed them down like shots of

Jägermeister. Brandon instantly creamed his jeans for what was possibly the 20th time in the past few hours, his knees going weak, the veins in his neck bulging out. He took a deep and contented breath. Stepped over so that he was looking directly up at Déjà. Tears fell from her eyes like raindrops.

"Why are you doing this, Brandon?"

"It's nothing personal, you know that, right?" The way he said it sounded almost sincere. Almost sympathetic. Déjà couldn't tell if he was acting or not. If anything he said was the truth or a lie. "It's not easy out there, little darling. Not even for someone like me. There are a hundred thousand people waiting to take my place. There always have been and always will be. I'm just doing what is necessary to keep my edge. I'm sure if the tables were turned, you'd do the same."

"No. I'm not like you," she said. "I'm not a monster."

"I suppose you're not." Brandon looked at his empty cup and licked out the last few drops. "Which is exactly why you're so darn *yummy*."

She could see him going for his pants again, the little pop tent on the front of his trousers fully erect and ready to blow. This was it. Her last chance. While he was distracted. Brandon stroked himself off with jackhammer speed. She had about six seconds to make her move.

So once more, she pulled with all her might. Muscles ground against bone. Pain rode up her arm. She could feel unconsciousness rushing up to greet her but she managed to push it back. With an audible *crunch* she finally wrenched her wrist free, and in one clean motion, smashed Brandon in the face with her bloody, raw nub.

It wasn't a hard blow. Even on her best day Déjà had only a fraction of the leading man's strength. But the sudden jab to his jaw came so fast and so unexpectedly that he had no time to put up a defense.

She made contact. His arms windmilled around as he toppled backward into the Marybelle and Charlie. The two of them were caught off guard too and knocked aside like bowling pins. A perfect strike.

And Brandon windmilled further. Momentum careened him out of control. Dr. Fish tried to get out of the way but with all the blood and pus and cum everywhere, he was unable to find his footing. The plastic surgeon lost his balance, and he alongside Brandon Bowers skidded into the extraction device. The machine tipped over with a thunderous crash.

The needle was instantly ripped out of Déjà's side. Apart from the single inky bubble still leaking from the puncture wound, the Reno stopped flowing.

The container on the side of the machine cracked open when it hit the ground and nearly a gallon of purple fluid spilled out onto the floor. Charlie and Marybelle and Brandon dropped to their knees and began lapping at the puddle's edge without hesitation, three wild animals in a feeding frenzy, adrenochrome all over their faces, soaking into their clothes.

Déjà whipped her free arm around and pressed the stump against the buckle on the opposite wrist. She wedged the brass clasp as deep as she could into the folds of her ruined flesh. More pain. Tidal waves of pain. Jerking her stump left and right, up and down, she managed to loosen the fastening and free her other arm.

She undid the straps around her ankles. Then the one around her waist. Gravity took over from there and she fell to the ground with a *thunk* next to the three feral A-listers.

For a moment, everyone froze. All parties surprised by her newfound freedom. Brandon stopped shoveling the Reno into his gullet and wiped his mouth with the back of his hand, smearing the adrenochrome further.

His gaze drifted toward the back of the room before returning to Déjà. She followed his line of sight. There was a door, almost invisible, the same color as the wall. Her escape, her salvation, only a few paces away.

Brandon sat up a little straighter. Marybelle licked her

STARLET

fingers clean like they were covered in blackberry jam. From behind Charlie's sunglasses, she could hear the tittering of his multiple mouths. Not only did nobody make a move for her, but to her surprise, Brandon nodded to the exit instead.

"Well, what are you waiting for?" he said. "Run, bitch! RUN! RUN! RUN! RUN!"

CHAPTER FIVE

MAUSOLEUM

(2012)
DIR. BY ROLAND EMMERICH

" . . . another lifeless CGI mess of a film, though I suppose we should be thankful that Hollywood is putting this kind of bloated budget behind an original IP instead of another remake or reboot. Of course, if this is what they're offering as an alternative, I'd rather have three more Mr. Ed sequels, thankyouverymuch. Front and center in this sci-fi action epic (and I'm using the term 'epic' loosely here) is wunderkind-turned-warm bowl of vanilla pudding, Brandon Bowers. Mausoleum—a story about an army of six-legged alien ghost bugs from Europa (pick a lane, Emmerich, jeesh) looking to turn all the moons in the Solar System into one big supermoon, because . . . reasons?—was intended to kick off a whole extended cinematic universe, with Bowers at the helm. Unfortunately, both in its construction and execution, the movie is a complete nonstarter, and Bowers' weak attempts to wink at the audience come across here as either lazy or cloying. I'm sorry, sir, but Dwayne Johnson you are not, and this film is poised to be yet another box-office blow for this rapidly dimming star. And while Bowers, who long ago burned through all his early-career buzz, might still be considered a draw to some, he has yet to attach himself to the kind of project that would solidify his celebrity in the zeitgeist beyond a quick talking point on Entertainment Tonight . . . "

DÉJÀ BURST OUT of the operating room, the door slamming shut behind her. There was nothing to barricade it with, nothing to stop her pursuers once they chose to pursue. As she fled down this long, dimly-lit hall, she could still hear them laughing. Calling her name. Mocking her. *Run bitch, run!* So clear it was like they were right in her ear. As if the walls themselves were laughing. As if the house were alive.

Years ago, back in Eau Claire, she had a black Bombay cat named Godiva, a skinny little panther with defiant yellow eyes and limitless energy. Every evening, the field mice would come out of their hidey-holes in the backyard to feed. And every evening, Godiva would show up in the backyard too, forever on the prowl, looking to tear those tiny mice apart. Déjà would be in her bedroom, reading a book or watching TV, and she could hear them. Her cat mewling. The terrified mice squeaking. All of it happening somewhere beyond the safety of the porch. Sometimes she'd go out and see what all the commotion was. She'd grab a flashlight and trudge through the grass, until she invariably came upon her kitty, pouncing on the defenseless rodent. Biting it. Shaking it around. Throwing it up in the air and letting it fall back down to the ground. Godiva the mighty hunter, beholden only to her cat-like nature. This wasn't about food. This wasn't about protection. To Godiva, this was all just a game. And after each act of violence, the mouse would stagger an escape, broken-legged, crooked-tailed, intestines spilling out of its side. Godiva would take a moment to appreciate her own handiwork before bringing it back over with a lazy swipe of the paw. The mouse must have known it stood no chance against a predator so large, and still, it took every opportunity it could to try and run, until it finally keeled over, able to run no more.

DANGER SLATER

Déjà didn't know where she was or where she was going. She was in some kind of labyrinth in the basement of the Bowers estate, as helpless as a rodent herself.

The hallway twisted and turned. Then split in two. Then twisted and turned again. Then split in two again. Déjà chose her route without discretion. Left. Right. Left. Sometimes she would hit an abrupt dead end, a blank wall, plastered and painted and leaving her nowhere else to go. So she'd double-back and head the other way, trying to keep a mental note of which direction she'd been.

Footsteps followed her throughout. Brandon and his friends getting closer. Or maybe it was just the sound of her own feet as she ran. In these claustrophobic corridors it was nearly impossible to tell.

She passed a door. Tried the handle. Locked.

Further down, another door. Tried that handle. Locked too.

The third door she passed she assumed would be locked as well, but when she turned the knob, it offered no resistance. Without a second thought, she ducked inside.

The room was done up, bright and colorful. Glossy pastel pinks and matte mint greens, with a soft beige carpet tickling her bare toes. As incongruous as it seemed, Déjà realized where she was immediately: a children's nursery, hidden amid this maze of passageways.

Did Brandon have a baby, she wondered? A secret lovechild? No, perhaps not. Something about this room was wrong. The dimensions were off. The furniture. The bottle. All the scattered toys. Things were too exaggerated. Too large. As if they were designed to be used by someone much taller than an infant.

A mobile hung from the ceiling like a chandelier, cartoon rocket ships dangling from the ends, chasing each other in a circle as a couple of high-pitched notes chimed. *Twinkle, Twinkle, Little Star*. Ratty stuffed animals sat piled up to the side like some kind of plushy mountain and a giant crib was positioned along the wall, large enough to fit a "baby" bigger than Déjà herself. A basket full of soiled cloth diapers filled the air with a feculent stench, and next to the changing station, some Polaroid pictures were scattered.

Déjà walked over. Picked one of the pictures up. A shot of Brandon Bowers, shirtless, in a bib and sucking on a binky, wearing a loaded diaper, drooping down to his knees, with a dark brown boom-boom leaking out of the backside, running down his inner thighs like chocolate fondue. A leather-clad mistress stood over him, ready to powder his butt and clean up his mess.

This truly was a house of horror.

"What if it's awkward?" Déjà asked her friend earlier that afternoon. "What if Brandon turns out to be an asshole? What if we don't get along? What if he doesn't like me?"

Déjà had already discussed what she was planning on wearing tonight. Which color lipstick and which pair of shoes. Now she was nervously chewing on the insides of her cheeks and trying not to unravel before the evening began.

Val laid a reassuring hand on Déjà's shoulder. "And what if he turns out to be the LOVE of your LIFE? What if this 'date' tonight is the best thing to ever happen to you?"

They were on a cigarette break. The fifth one for Déjà in the last three hours. She normally didn't smoke this much. She hardly ever smoked at all. But she was anxious and it gave her something to do.

"Shit, I don't think I've ever seen anyone so starstruck in my whole life," said Val. "What happened to the cool and confident Déjà from yesterday?"

"She's taking the afternoon off," Déjà replied. "Meet her *uncool* and *not-so-confident* doppelganger."

Val tossed her Parliament Full Flavor to the pavement and stomped it out with the tip of her toe. "Look, Dé, I know I've been pushing you with this Bowers thing. It's been exciting for me too, vicariously-speaking."

"I don't know if I'd call it *pushing* so much as *gently shaming* . . . "

"Listen, I'm being serious now. I want you to be careful, okay? You gotta get your head on straight. I don't want you walking into a situation you can't walk out of."

"Val . . . "

"This town is all about appearances, Dé. All the glitz and glamour, distracting you from the darkness festering underneath."

Déjà rolled her eyes. "Okay, now you sound like my mother . . . "

"Shut up. I'm just tryin'ta look out for a friend, alright? I ain't saying that Brandon Bowers is trouble. Even with all those weird thirsty DMs—that whole meat-fucking thing—I ain't implying anything untoward. We all got our quirks. Who am I to judge? Shit, for all I know, Bowers might be more wholesome than St. Keanu himself. I just want you to remember, how people act and who people are can sometimes be two very different beasts."

"C'mon Val. I'm not some wilting flower. And if I'm being totally honest here, Brandon's motives are the least of my concerns. In the end, this night is all about *me*. About what I want outta life. What I can prove. This is my *opportunity*. And I'm not about to let it pass me by."

"Fair point, but still, that's a bit cynical, don'tcha think, Dé? I mean, you're *using* him, if you wanna get right down to it."

"Some people look at success like it's some impossible or unobtainable thing. Dumb luck. Destiny. Whatever. But I've never believed that. Life is like a series of doors, each one leading to some unknown other room. You can stay where you are. Stay with what's safe. Or you can conjure up the guts and charge ahead until you've reached the other side."

Val considered this for a moment and then offered her

friend what seemed like the most obvious rebuttal. "But what if you don't like what's on the other side?"

Déjà brushed her off with a wave of the hand. "You know, last week you were telling me to send him pictures of myself dry-humping a porterhouse steak, and now you're telling me I might be going too far?"

"Déjà, I ain't telling you shit. In fact, I get the feeling that no one has ever been able to tell you nothing. I'm just saying, you stick your head too far out of the chicken coop and the farmer is liable to chop it clean off. WHACK! Then you're nothing but nuggets. Battered and fried."

Déjà couldn't help but laugh. "That is the stupidest fucking metaphor I've ever heard in my life, Val."

Val laughed too. "Yeah, guess it was, huh? I think I'm just hungry. You wanna grab some In-N-Out before we go back?"

"Make it a salad and you got yourself a deal."

Back in the hallway, direction lost all meaning. Left. Right. Forward. Backward. Repeat. Déjà was scrambling. Becoming more desperate with every disorienting turn. The stump at the end of her wrist dripped globs of flesh onto the floor, leaving a trail of bloody breadcrumbs for the hooting celebrities to follow. She could hear them. Brandon and Marybelle and Charlie. Dr. Fish too. A drunken parade, filling up the space around her.

Another dead end. Back around. To another. And then one more. She was running out of options. The walls were closing in, growing tighter, like some kind of giant esophagus trying to swallow her down, deeper into its belly. Were she to stop moving, she'd surely be digested.

And adrenaline continued to charge through her veins in much the same way she charged through the passageways. Haphazardly. Chaotically. Frantically searching for a way out. Fear so palpable she was boiling alive in it, made even more terrifying by the knowledge that this was exactly what Brandon and his compatriots wanted. The same influx of adrenaline that kept her going was exactly the reason they were terrorizing her in the first place. Like Dr. Fish said, fight or flight. She was a mouse. He was Godiva. This was all just a game to him, yet she had no choice but to keep moving, until the bitter end.

And eventually, Déjà found herself with no more labyrinth to walk through. No more hallways to double-back on. No other places left to go. Before her stretched one long corridor. The final corridor. Ushering her onward toward the final door.

If there was a way out of here, this had to be it.

She pushed her way through.

Unlike the nursery, the room she now found herself in was poorly lit and as cold as a refrigerator. Déjà could see her breath, a faint cloud in front of her, dissipating into the surrounding shadow. A single overhead light dangled by a string, casting the room in a David Fincher-esque palette of washed-out industrial-looking blues.

Another door sat along the opposite wall. The only way out. The only path forward. Impossible to get to without being detected by the murky figure in the center of the room, hunched over a metal table, too engrossed in the task before it to notice she had entered.

From where she stood, Déjà could hear what the figure was doing better than she could see it. The grinding teeth of a handsaw gave way to a celery-like crack. The figure exchanged the saw in its hand for a cleaver and started hacking away. *Thwack. Squish. Thwack. Squish.* Like a butcher in the backroom of a deli.

On the tips of her toes, she made her way toward the exit. Behind the hum of the air conditioner, she remained unheard. Beyond the halo of light, she moved unseen.

STARLET

A second crack from the table. Unquestionably the breaking of a bone. Déjà could hardly believe her eyes as the scene finally came into view. The figure wresting the ribcage free from the torso of what she could now see was a splayed human corpse.

She instinctively recoiled and was struck between the shoulder blades by something cold and hard. She spun around and was greeted by her own haggard reflection, almost unrecognizable—wild-eyed, frazzle-haired, mono-handed, bloody-nosed—cast back at her a dozen times over in a collection of chrome, forearm-shaped handles.

Each handle was attached to a coffin-sized cabinet. And these coffin-sized cabinets made up the entirety of the back wall.

This was a morgue, Déjà realized. Brandon Bowers kept an entire morgue in the basement of his mansion. And the person wrenching pieces from the cadaver in the middle of the room—the shock of silver in her curly hair, white apron now peppered with droplets of red—was Brandon's maid, Alice.

Alice snapped the leg off the mutilated body on the table, the bone fractured in such a way that it stuck out of the top of the calf. She split the muscle. Peeled away the flesh. Placed the knife-like femur alongside the other organs and body parts she'd removed, lined up like the entrees at some kind of ghastly buffet.

The stink of rot pervaded everything. Noxious. Nauseating.

But Déjà was not deterred. She took a silent step. And another. Closing in on the exit. Just a few yards away.

"I know you're there, Ms. Seawright." The middle-aged woman laid down her tools and peered over her shoulder. Her voice was calm. Unsurprised by the intrusion. "Come on out now, child. No use creepin' around in the dark like a cockroach."

Déjà ambled out of the shadow, her one good hand up in surrender. "Please don't kill me."

"I don't kill people." Alice reached back into the open cadaver, a young woman, from what Déjà could tell, though it was difficult to make out any of her features besides her tangle of curly blonde hair and a small tattoo on her upper bicep of a peace symbol. The maid grabbed onto something and pulled it free. She held up a purplish bean-shaped object. "I'm just the hired help."

"Who was she?" asked Déjà.

"Nobody," Alice replied.

The corpse was still fresh, relatively-speaking. The guts still squished when Alice dug around inside them. She pulled out a second purple bean.

Kidneys, thought Déjà, before noting the fatty little pouch located on the top—the adrenal gland—which Alice now pared with the exacting precision of a jeweler.

"It takes a lotta work to get 'em just right," said Alice. "It's kinda like *foie gras*, like how they force feed the goose to get its liver nice and plump. Same basic principle. Sometimes it only takes a few hours. Sometimes a few days. Sometimes a month or more. Everybody is different. Fear is such a personal thing."

"Why are you doing this?"

"I told you, it's my job."

"But you're not like them."

"Not like them?"

"You're not *famous*."

"No I'm not, but that don't make me a fool either. The world ain't gonna hand you roses just 'cause you like the smell of flowers. I always thought it'd be nice to be a movie star myself. Almost went for it too, once upon a time." Alice gave a quick glance to the bifurcated body before her. "Sometimes you just gotta accept your station. Accept who and what you are. Some of us only get to play bit parts in life. But we all gotta survive."

For a fleeting moment, Déjà thought Alice looked more like her mother than ever, the same forced smile on her weathered face, the same tired bags sat under her sad glassy eyes.

"You can come with me." Déjà nodded to the door. "You probably know this house better than anyone. You can show me the way. We can get out of here. Together."

A glimmer of consideration flashed across the maid's face, but she ultimately shook her head no. "I don't think it's going to be that easy, Ms. Seawright."

"Please. Imani. That is your real name, isn't it? Imani? Well my real name is Dorothy. Dorothy Smalls. You don't have to do this, Imani. You don't have to participate in their sick game. You don't have to hurt me. Imani, please . . . "

"Stop calling me that." Alice clenched her teeth, nearly shaking with rage. "Stop telling me who I am. You're young and stupid and you don't know shit. You can't just walk in here and expect to walk out again. We all have our roles. That's how it works."

The maid turned to a nearby intercom and hit the call button. Déjà could do nothing to stop her. It chirped only once before someone picked up on the other end.

"She's with me, Mr. Bowers," said Alice. "In the morgue."

Through the speaker, Brandon's voice crackled. "Two minutes."

Click.

Alice turned back to Déjà. "Hope you had a nice evening, but Mr. Bowers is a very busy man with a very busy schedule, and unfortunately for you, we'll have to be ending the night a tad prematur—"

Déjà had heard enough. She grabbed the femur bone off the table and smacked the maid on the head with it so hard it sounded like a pistol went off.

Alice stood there for a moment, silently blinking, too stunned to move, too stunned to even speak, only registering what had happened to her when a sheet of blood started to cascade out of the fissure in her skull.

Déjà was almost too stunned to react as well. She'd never hit someone so hard before. She was surprised she was capable of it.

Alice let loose an unearthly and homicidal yowl as she lurched in Déjà's direction.

The two ladies stumbled backward, into the table, knocking the dead body and all of its assorted parts to the floor. Underfoot, the pile of organs were rendered into jelly. Both kidneys ruptured like overripe plums. The adrenal glands turned to pulp between Déjà's toes.

Alice screamed. Bled. Clamped onto Déjà's windpipe and wouldn't let go. Déjà slipped and slid through the human slop, only able to gain the slightest bit of traction after sticking her foot into the chest hole of the corpse itself. She pushed with all her might. Alice stumbled backward, into one of the mortuary cabinets, striking the side of her head in the process. She immediately went cross-eyed and loosened her grasp. Déjà wasn't about to take any chances, though. She slammed Alice's head into the handle again. And again and again and again. Until the skull of the maid was nothing but paste.

Déjà opened the cabinet and shoved the limp housekeeper into the darkness. The electrical twitch of those final few nerve cells firing sounded for a moment like Alice knocking to be let out. But a few seconds later that stopped as well.

Déjà wanted to stop and catch her breath, but this was no time to relax. Brandon knew where she was. And he was on his way.

She picked up the sharpened femur bone, tucked it into the back of her skirt, and took off.

CHAPTER SIX

EGGS WITH A SIDE OF HOPE

(2013)
DIR. BY NANCY APPLEBAUM & GERRY MARSH

" . . . now it should be said that I'm typically not in the habit of railing against a film, regardless of quality. Every movie is a tiny miracle, and all art deserves a fair shake when it comes to criticism and critique. That said, the failure of Eggs with a Side of Hope is so in-your-face, so unequivocal, that it's almost transcendent; the kind of cathartic box-office bomb we only get to see play out every once in a gray while. It's Gigli. It's Battlefield Earth. It's John Carter redux. Eggs with a Side of Hope is the story of a small-town waitress who is granted angel-like powers after a near-death experience with a malfunctioning microwave, for whom things get further complicated when she falls for a corporate liaison looking to replace her folksy diner (and by extension ALL folksy diners) with an IHOP-esque breakfast food chain. The plot here is not only insultingly banal, but also poorly executed on nearly every level. The look of the film. The soundtrack. The entire conceit. All of it is at odds, and none of it works. But beyond the flat camerawork and ridiculously saccharine script, perhaps the biggest disappointment for this reviewer comes by way of the performances. Both Brandon Bowers and Marybelle Ashton are downright off-putting as the two romantic leads. For stars of their caliber, they are a shockingly unappealing onscreen couple. I've honestly seen more chemistry in a middle school science class. Ashton, perhaps, can be forgiven. This kind of movie is well within her purview, and we've seen these kinds of high-concept/low-effort rom-coms from her before. But Bowers? Not so much. This might come as the final nail in the coffin for the once-promising A-lister; the latest in a run of big-budgeted, high-profile flops . . . "

THE DOOR SWUNG shut and disappeared seamlessly into the wall. No cracks. No handle. Not a single blemish in the paint. You couldn't even tell a door had been there. The hallways, the morgue, the nursery, the surgical suite and observation deck were all reabsorbed back into the deeper bowels of the house. And Déjà now found herself in some sort of parlor, decked out and designed to resemble the atrium of a grand old theater.

Empire chandeliers hung elegantly from the high ceiling above. A plush red carpet lay gently beneath her bloody red feet. Gilded rococo furniture was placed sparsely throughout. A fire crackled in a fireplace on the far side of the room, where golden bands of light danced with the thin shadows cast by the banister of a staircase.

Déjà had no idea how many levels down they had taken her, but she knew she had to go up to get out, no matter where these stairs might lead.

Running was no longer an option for her, but she could still hobble and she could still hop, and toward the staircase she hobbled and hopped along, taking in the rows of photographs that hung upon the walls. There were too many to count in a single glance, dozens if not hundreds of framed 8x10s, evenly spaced apart to create a gallery of sorts. To Déjà's left, the headshot of a smiling young woman. Slim. Beautiful. In her early 20s.

To her right, another headshot, similar to the first. Another smiling young woman. Also slim. Also beautiful. Also in her early 20s.

In fact, all of these photos could fit this exact description. Actress after actress, hung on the wall. Names she didn't recognize. Faces she couldn't place. Going down the line, until there was one that stood out, with curly blonde hair. She had such a sparkle in her eye, looking so hopeful, so affable, so ready to take on the world.

And she also had a small peace sign tattoo on her upper bicep.

This was a photograph of the girl from the morgue. The one that Alice was chopping apart. A shudder climbed Déjà's spine as it occurred to her what she was looking at.

This wasn't an art gallery. It was a trophy room.

And indeed, across from the headshot of the blonde was a headshot of Déjà, her name and contact information written across the bottom, the expression on her face as inviting and as approachable as she could possibly project. This was the same headshot she had printed up her first week in LA. The one that she had sent to casting agents. The one she put on the top of her near-empty IMDb page.

How many girls had come before her? How many would come after she was gone?

And looming over this entire macabre exhibition was a gigantic hand-painted portrait of Brandon Bowers himself, standing larger than life, nearly 15 feet tall, hearkening back to those ubiquitous old billboards that launched his career nearly two decades ago.

In the painting, his foot was on top of a felled elephant, with a blunderbuss resting cockily on his hip, like an extension of his meager manhood, which was also exposed. The tiny tip of his dick stuck out of the fly of his safari pants, a little fleshy button. Despite herself, Déjà couldn't help but wonder why he didn't have the artist embellish his bits. Or at least make them proportional to the rest of this body. As it were, his crotch was the focal point of the entire portrait, casting a peculiar type of energy around which everything else in the room seemed to revolve, as if his dick were some kind of miniature Lovecraftian divining rod, calling forth a madness that would subjugate all those who gazed upon it.

Or maybe Brandon just got off on making people look at his weird malformed dong. Hard to say.

A sudden *sssssscreaking* caught Déjà's attention. She whipped around just as the hidden door from the mortuary unsealed itself. They must have discovered what she did to Alice and their latest adrenal gland harvest. Voices could be heard, no longer laughing. They sounded angry. They were coming for her.

She knew she'd never be able to make it up the stairs in time. Not in the state she was in. But a slender wooden door sat to the side of the painting, which Déjà figured must have been some kind of broom closet or storage space. It was a stupid place to hide but she had little recourse. Whatever it was, and wherever it led, she stepped inside and quickly closed it behind her, disappearing into the dark.

Though it was impossible to see anything, Déjà could tell the room was much larger than a broom closet, and yet, it was mostly empty. It had the same kind of echo her Van Nuys apartment had when she first moved in—sleeping on a pile of blankets on the floor. Watching movies on her laptop using her neighbor's unprotected Wi-Fi signal. A peanut butter and jelly sandwich, cut into quarters, to be eaten sporadically throughout the day. She had to not only watch her wallet but also watch her weight. She counted her calories. She tracked her daily steps. She was a blank slate. A brand-new woman in a brand-new life, refusing to carry with her any baggage from her past.

Beyond her panicked breaths, she could hear something else. Some kind of sonorous whirr. The sound of bubbles. The muted splash of displaced water.

Hands out, grasping at the nothingness, Déjà stumbled around until she found the wall. Working in a small but efficient pattern, she moved her palm up and down, left and right, before finding what she was looking for. A light switch. She flicked it on.

Blue light surrounded her, cerulean and soft, not coming from a lamp or overhead fixture, but from inside the saltwater aquarium that took up the entire back half of the room, from ceiling to the ground.

A medium-sized shark clocked Déjà immediately and started to swim around in hungry and hypnotizing circles, its obsidian black eyes never leaving hers.

"It's a mako," a velvety voice behind her said. "As metaphors go, perhaps it's a tad on the nose. But I like the aesthetics."

Brandon was already in the room, the door already reshut, just the two of them, trapped beneath the sea. She pulled the sharpened bone out of her waistband. The femur of a peace-sign tattooed ingénue was her last and only line of defense. "Stay back!"

Brandon innocently held up his hands and offered her the same ineffable smile that drew her to him in the first place. "Okay. It's okay. We're just talking, alright?"

"So then talk. Tell me what the hell all this is all about. And no more rambling speeches like that fucking *doctor* or whatever he is."

He nodded toward the tank. "Take a closer look."

Her eyes darted to the water, then back to him, not sure if this was some kind of trick to distract her. She had nowhere to run and no place to hide.

"Go on," Brandon said. "No funny business. I promise. You certainly have the LEG UP in this situation. Haha. Get it? Leg up? Cause you're holding a leg bone? That was an ad-lib, by the way. No good? We can go again. Ready? *ahem* 'No funny business. I promise to TOE the line.' Guess that second one wasn't as punchy, but you get the picture."

Déjà squinted into the tank. Surrounding the mako shark were hundreds of tiny bulbous jellyfish, bobbing around aimlessly, semi-translucent and so small they were almost invisible, save for the light shining through their bodies, which made the cloudy water shimmer with an otherworldly hue.

"*Turritopsis dohrnii*," Brandon said. "The immortal jellyfish, to be precise."

STARLET

"The immortal jellyfish?"

"Biological speaking, of course. Unique in the animal kingdom. No brain to speak of. No lungs. No heart. Just a tangle of nerve endings, clumped together into a ball of diaphanous goo. Surely, one of God's most frivolous and unloved creatures, totally useless, except for one remarkable feature: the T. dohrnii can evade threat by reverting back to their polyp stage and reattaching themselves to the ocean floor. Whereas a possum under duress might be inclined to play dead, when the T. dohrnii is threatened it will instead play *unborn*. They shed their aging tissue, shed all their unwanted parts, and sink to the safety of the bottom of the sea. And once the danger has passed, the Dohrnii will start its life cycle anew. Fresh cells. Fresh flesh. You see where I'm going with this, don't you, Déjà? All we had to do was pinpoint the specific mRNA sequence responsible for regeneration, synthesize it, tweak it to fit the human genome, and voilà!"

"Eternal youth," she muttered under her breath. Brandon nodded in the affirmative.

"DohrniiTox is what the Good Doctor calls it. That's propitiatory, by the way. A secret formula. Patent pending. And before you even ask, I don't know how it works exactly. And more importantly, I really don't care. A DohrniiTox shot every few months with a steady supply of Reno to jump-start the regeneration process. More effective than Botox. Certainly more effective than plastic surgery. From Paul Rudd to Jennifer Lopez to Jared Leto. We're not just LOOKING younger, little darling. We're STAYING younger too."

"This is insane."

"I know, it sounds like the plot of one of my movies, doesn't it?"

"So you cultivate and harvest the adrenochrome from young actresses like me . . . ?"

" . . . and we use it to activate the DohrniiTox treatments given to us by Dr. Fish. You got it."

"But I saw all three of you turn into monsters. You didn't become *younger*. You became *something else*."

"Oh that. Just a minor and temporary side effect as the Reno takes hold. Gotta jettison the old cells to remold the new ones. DNA is a fragile thing. It's all about mitigation and management. Those are the keys to a happy and healthy life. Take my . . . *premature ejaculations*, for instance." He motioned down to his crotch. "Think of 'em like releasing the spit valve on a trombone. Except, ya know, with excess jelly buildup instead of saliva. Helps keep the pipes clear. Helps me keep my head on straight."

"But why go through all this trouble?" she said. "Why not just . . . *get older*, like people do? Like everyone does? Why turn yourself into this FREAK of NATURE?"

Brandon laughed, hearty and loud. His hands no longer up, clearly only humoring her with his moment of surrender. The two of them kept a wide berth between them as they circled around the room, the Moon and the Earth, locked into place.

"It's not *me*," Brandon said. "It's the industry. It's this whole damn town. I'm no more the bad guy than the shark in that tank is a bad fish. I mean, think about it. I am an *actor*. I bring joy into people's lives. I entertain millions. I am a force of good in the world, little darling, even if I *still* don't have all the accolades I need to prove it . . . "

She could see him grinding his teeth. Starting to sweat. He pulled a small glass vial out of his pocket, unscrewed the cap, and stuck it in his nostril. He inhaled the Reno inside in one loud, honking snort. His pupils turned to dinner plates. He continued.

" . . . I mean, not to keep harping on this, but seriously, where the FUCK is my Oscar, huh? What the hell is wrong with the Academy? They gave one to Casey Affleck for God's sake. Casey Affleck! I can act the pants off of Casey fucking Affleck! You've seen *The Perfect Gentleman*, right? 89% on Rotten Tomatoes. Well, that was me. *I* was the perfect gentleman. No one else could've pulled off that role, and guess what? No one else did."

He was further unraveling. Ranting. Raving. His body unfolded out of itself, like a spume of seafoam unable to fight the tide. His eyebrows once again slid down his face, settling on his cheeks. His hunched back swelled up so big it overtook most of his head. His false teeth fell out like overcooked kernels of corn. Warts and lesions appeared on his skin, and his nose doubled in length, like Pinocchio suddenly caught in a lie.

"Goddamn it, can't you people see that I am a compassionate and caring individual?! That's what makes me such a good actor in the first place. I am full of empathy." He looked like a Picasso, his exaggerated features out of place. Undoubtedly, the flurry of emotion he was experiencing and expressing was having an adverse effect on his body, sending parts akimbo. "Everybody knows I'm a bleeding-heart liberal, like all of the Hollywood greats. I am doing exactly what I'm supposed to do. I give money to UNICEF and Breast Cancer Awareness. I try to use my platform and privilege to inform the masses about the vital social issues plaguing our society today. There is so much injustice in the world. I mean, Black people have it pretty rough out there, in case you haven't heard, and apparently it's been bad for them for a really long time. Well, I want to end racism! I want to save the whales! I want to put a stop to the production of single-use plastics! Sure, it's been a personal struggle for me as an artist, trying to stay relevant over the years. And I know once you're on top, the only place left to go is down. And I suppose, on the surface, the measures my friends and I have taken to help extend our shelf life may seem extreme. But as far as the public is concerned, and all things being equal, my continued success is a NET POSITIVE for all of humankind. So if you can't see that, then you can't see the big picture. They say you only get so many bites of the apple. They say that time marches on. They say that occasionally new blood is needed to replace the old. Well, excuse me, but fuck that. I refuse to give up. I refuse to step aside. I will bite the apple as many goddamn times as I want. I will take what is rightfully mine, and I'll take it by force if I have to. Because it's not simply enough to LIVE forever, little darling. I demand to be LOVED forever too."

Brandon looked at her imploringly, as if his little diatribe were supposed to inspire a standing ovation or something. Instead, Déjà held the sharpened bone in front of her with a trembling hand, a makeshift dagger she had no idea how to wield.

Brandon ran an exhausted hand through his slimy hair. "You can put that down. We both know you're not going to stab me with it."

"Maybe you're right." Déjà looked at the bone. "But also, that was never my plan."

And she swung the femur at the side of the tank beside her, forcing the pointed end into the glass as hard and as deep as she possibly could.

Spiderweb cracks quickly crawled across the pane, going *tink tink tink* as it gave way to the pressure. A single leak sprung. Then several leaks. And within seconds, the whole side of the aquarium exploded outward. A deluge of jellyfish water poured into the room, taking the mako along for the ride. The shark rushed by Brandon, jaws chomping up and down. The actor pulled back just in time to avoid having his head bit off.

Under the weight of the seawater, the door buckled too. Brandon, Déjà, and the shark spilled out into the atrium, an unexpected tsunami that swept the rest of the waiting celebrities off their feet.

"What the fuck?!" Dr. Fish cried out as the shark sunk its razor-sharp teeth into the side of his ribs. He tried to fight it off but the shark was too fast, tearing through the crinkled flesh of the aging plastic surgeon in an instant. Intestines like a landslide burbled out of the wound. His once-white coat turned pink with blood and bodily debris.

STARLET

Brandon snatched up the femur and speared the mako shark through the top of its head, piercing its brain. One final thrash was all the apex predator could muster before the life flickered out of its eyes.

"Dr. Fish?" The soaking-wet Marybelle stood up and tapped the doctor with her foot. He wasn't moving. Wasn't breathing. Was only half intact. Was already dead.

Brandon placed a gentle hand on his former co-star's shoulder. "Yeah, I don't think he's going to make it, MB."

"Not gonna make it?" Marybelle's eyes were wide with panic. "But if there's no more Dr. Fish that means there's no more DohrniiTox either, right?"

"I think I still have one dose left upstairs," Brandon replied.

"ONE DOSE?! Are you kidding me? That's not gonna work. What about next month? And what about the month after that?"

"I know."

"So what the fuck are we supposed to do now?"

"I don't know."

"Well we're rich, aren't we? That's gotta count for something. Bad things don't happen to rich people."

"Uh . . . yeah . . . maybe . . . "

"Goddamn it." Marybelle kicked the dead shark out of frustration. "Where the hell is she, Brandon? Where did that little bitch run off to?"

"I'm not sure. She must have slipped away in all the confusion."

Charlie cleared his throat and pointed to the staircase. "Onward and upward, would be my guess," he said. "Though I wish I would've known we'd be fighting sharks tonight, I would've worn my Canali suit and not the Brioni."

CHAPTER SEVEN

ECHO CHAMBER

(2015)
DIR. BY W. ERIKSON OFFERDAHL

" . . . at odds with the excessively schmaltzy material, Bowers' weirdly-pitched performance not only fails to elevate this story, but openly detracts from it. Perhaps this is partially due to a memorable turn from John Lithgow as the dementia-suffering patriarch of the Chambers family, a clear standout in yet another by-the-numbers 'inspirational' faux-arthouse drama that we see studios annually unleash as we creep up on award season. As far as shameless Oscar bait goes, Echo Chamber is clearly the most egregious of this year's crop . . . "

DÉJÀ EMERGED FROM the middle door between the superfluous dual pantries. Finally out of the basement. Back to the main floor of the house.

She limped over to the island and rifled through the drawers, looking for something to defend herself with. A knife. A pair of scissors. Anything. The closest she came up with was a vegetable peeler. Unless Brandon secretly had potato DNA in him too, this was not going to work.

"You really fucked up, you know that, right?"

Brandon stood in the doorway to the basement, arm upon the frame, clenching and unclenching his fist, knuckles recracking every time. Though his voice was calm she could sense the rage like magma bubbling just under the exterior.

"First Alice. Then Dr. Fish. Maybe I underestimated you, little darling. You jammed a big ole monkey wrench into our well-oiled machine. Dr. Fish was the best in the business. The Surgeon to the Stars™, lest you forget." He took a slow step into the room. She squeezed the potato peeler in her hand. He saw it and scoffed. "Might take us a minute to find a new doctor. Maybe we can talk Jake Gyllenhaal's physician into picking up where Fish left off? Might need to shoot him a text. Regardless, until this all gets straightened out, it appears that YOU are our only source of Reno for the foreseeable future." He lowered his gaze, intimidating. "You've only experienced a fraction of what we're going to do to you, little darling. We are going to wring you dry. Nice and slow. Months, it'll take. Perhaps even years. Every waking moment from here on out will be a living nightmare. You'll wish you'd have died tonight as we squeeze from you every last delicious drop."

Brandon advanced. Déjà grabbed the refrigerator door and swung it open as hard as she could. It hit Brandon in the face and instantly broke his nose. The Rorschach pattern of blood on the stainless steel illustrated his surprise.

But her moment of triumph was short-lived when she caught a glimpse inside the open fridge. There were a dozen different body parts from a dozen different dead bodies in there. A half-eaten human foot, already starting to rot. Unnameable organs stored in Tupperware containers. A woman's head on a plate, skull cleaved open, spoon sticking out of the top like it was a bowl of gazpacho soup. The only non-human thing in the fridge that Déjà could see was the row of fancy French mustard bottles and a loaf of bread. All the ingredients Brandon needed for his "mustard meat sandwich." The smell was so powerful she almost passed out.

"Like I told you, I am 1/32nd Tongva Indian," the extraordinarily European-looking former billboard model said. "My people used every part of the buffalo. I take my heritage *very* seriously."

She grabbed the refrigerator door and swung it open again, clocking Brandon in the face once more. This time he fell over and landed hard. His hair was blown back and sat like an abandoned bird's nest on the top of his speckled dome, a toupee from which the glue came loose. A few of his false teeth were missing. He spat them out, three in a row.

"Great, now I gotta find a fucking *dentist* to get me some new dentures, too . . . "

Déjà took off. Out of the kitchen. Down the grand hallway. Vaulted ceiling above. Pentelic marble below. The front door in front of her. Outside. Getting closer. So close.

But before she could reach it, Charlie Eccentric stepped out from the side, his silver suit clung to his spindly limbs, a daddy-longlegs in designer duds.

Déjà skid to a stop. Charlie blocked her only way out.

Skeleton-thin fingers slipped into the front pocket of his blazer, where he produced a small glass vial identical to the one Brandon had in the aquarium. He popped off the cap, and in one big toot, inhaled the Reno within.

STARLET

He tittered like a crazed woodpecker as the Reno xylophoned its way through his body. He stood taller. Unfolded out of himself. Long lanky limbs grew lankier and longer.

He took off his sunglasses and tossed them aside. Eyes squinted into thin slits. Some kind of clear gelatinous fluid oozed out from under the lids. And when they reopened, they reopened as mouths. Tongues replaced his pupils. Crooked teeth stuck out of lips like lashes. A mist of drool shot out as these two extra orifices began to titter too. His face was an entire Greek chorus, laughing at her.

The exit was just a few steps away. But there would be no getting past the infamous pop artist. Spider and fly. He had long since set the trap.

So Déjà turned and fled the only other direction she could.

Up the spiral staircase.

To the second floor.

This was a terrible plan. This was remedial shit. Horror Movie Tropes 101 type shit. Scrambling up the stairs? Trapping herself on the second story? How many times had a scene like this played out before her on the big screen? How many times had she and her high school buddies sat in the theater frustratedly shouting at the main character like, 'What are you doing, you idiot?! The way out is behind you! Don't go upstairs, you fool!'

And yet here she was. The idiot. The fool. The way out behind her.

Déjà's severed wrist throbbed as the shock of her injury wore off and the soreness settled in. Every beat of her pounding heart only magnified her discomfort. All she wanted to do was close her eyes and sleep. Let oblivion take over. Let her never wake again.

And yet, she continued to limp forward, as she had

always done. Each footstep tore her nerves open anew. The carpet might as well have been broken glass.

There was a room at the end of the corridor. Brandon's bedroom, she assumed, what seemed like millions upon millions of miles away. Even if she were to reach it, what was she going to do? What was her plan? Put a lampshade over her head and spend the rest of her life pretending to be a lamp? Escape was untenable. All she was doing was delaying the inevitable. This was *exactly* where they wanted her. Adrenaline-ripe. Ready.

Charlie quickly caught up to her. He didn't even have to run. All of a sudden, there he was, sweeping the ground beneath her with his leg like he was the Karate fucking Kid. Déjà tumbled. Landed flat on her back.

There was a flash of blinding white light. For a second Déjà thought she struck her head, but no, she could hear the sound of a photograph ejecting itself from an instant camera. Another flash. A third. A fourth. Charlie Eccentric was standing over her, taking a succession of Polaroids.

"Yes!" His excited voice came out of all three mouths at once. *flash* *flash* Portraits like oak leaves fell down around her. "Authenticity! That's what I wanna see! That is the true essence of art!" *flash* "I want to preserve this moment, in all its illusive permutations. Hopelessness, like a single piano note played over and over and over again. And yet, upon your malleable face, we see that with each new photograph, with each passing second, there are a thousand subtle and heartbreakingly inspired ways to articulate the same general theme. Death comes for us all.

"So we'll line these pictures up, across the gallery. Stick 'em to the wall with thumbtacks or Scotch tape or something like that. A real low-fi setup. Real visceral. And the patrons will walk into the show and follow along. They will take this final and fatal journey with you, watching as your expression shifts in abject horror the closer and closer we get to your inevitable end. *Fear: An Evolution* is what I think I will call it. The kind of piece that dares to show us

who we *really* are when we have no place left to hide."
flash *flash* "Honestly, you're very photogenic, Dorothy
Smalls. A total natural. It's all in the eyes. You probably
would've made a great actress, had things played out a bit
differently. But oh well. At least a part of you can live
forever as my canvas tonight."

"Derivative . . . ".

Charlie lowered his camera. "What did you just say to
me?"

"Your work is derivative," Déjà repeated herself. "Using
Polaroid as an analog for both intimacy and
impermanence? The overexposed colors and low
resolution, like a memory in the process of being
forgotten? Warhol already explored this idea back in the
late 70s, using instant film to take portraits of all his
celebrity friends. Fame captured, both real and ethereal.
This is well-worn territory. Your look. Your persona. The
stupid statements you're making with your stupid art.
There is nothing original or exciting about it. Warhol was
doing all this while you were still potty training."

Charlie stared at her for a half-second, too shocked to
speak.

"No," he finally said. "No, that's not what I'm going for.
This is more of a postmodern take on the Warhol vibe. A
post-ironic kind of thing. Even my style is supposed to be
post-ironic. It's like . . . a commentary ON the commentary
of pop culture itself. I dress this way because this is the way
artists dress when people think of an artist. I am winking
to my audience but also sincerely embodying the role.
There are layers here, Dorothy. *Metatextual* layers. It's real
heady stuff, I'm sure you wouldn't get it."

"You're using kitsch as a transgression against the
notion of kitsch itself? Yeah, I think I get it. You jerked off
on a crucified frog. Very edgy. Very clever."

Again, he was flummoxed, as if he never really
considered this perspective before. "First off, it was a
tadpole and not a frog. And secondly, this isn't just kitsch.

The threat you're facing isn't a metaphor. At the end of the day, I really am going to kill you. So even you have to admit, there's a certain rawness to this whole endeavor, is there not? Perhaps you just need to reframe your point of view. Think of this moment as the dichotomy between aspiration and destruction, and how we allow ourselves to be torn apart by our own desires."

Déjà shrugged. "I just think your thesis is a bit *convoluted,* is all."

"Convoluted?!" Charlie was annoyed now. A trio of scowls sat upon his three sets of lips. "I'm sorry, but should I really be taking criticism from *you* of all people? What the hell do you know about fine art, anyway? You're just another country bumpkin clogging up the streets of Los Angeles like too much cholesterol. Another wannabe starlet from Nowheresville, USA. You're all the same, and you don't even know it. Did Mommy and Daddy used to tell you you were their special princess? Did your high school drama teacher cast you as Potiphar's Wife in *Joseph and the Amazing Technicolor Dreamcoat*? Who planted these stupid seeds in your stupid head, huh? You think you're gonna make it out here? You think you're any different than the rest of 'em? Better, somehow? More talented? Blessed by God himself? Look, Dorothy, I'm sure at one point you were the prettiest young lady in Pigfucker County, but you'd have to be delusional to think you could just pack your little car up and kiss your childhood kitty goodbye and drive all the way to Hollywood without having to confront the unavoidable truth. We're all hungry in this town. But only some of us get to eat."

Déjà cast her eyes defeatedly to the ground. "Maybe you're right. Maybe girls like me are a dime a dozen. Maybe I was stupid for believing otherwise. Maybe I won't make it, in the end." She looked back up, a sly smirk on her face. "And maybe I was just trying to distract you so I could kick you in the balls."

"Huh?"

And before Charlie had time to realize what was happening, she kicked him directly in the crotch as hard as she could. This was Fight Scene Tropes 101 type shit, no doubt. But it was a classic for a reason.

The pop artist *ouffed* and doubled over. Face beet red. Wind forced out of his lungs. He dropped to his knees, involuntarily bowing before her.

Déjà sprung into action. She crab-crawled until she was positioned behind him. She slipped out of her old jean jacket for the first time since the night began and wrapped it around his neck like a noose.

Gagging. Struggling. His hands moved from his nuts to his throat as he tried in vain to pry the denim loose. Déjà held it taut by the sleeves, her knee driven into his back for leverage, the knot constricting his airflow, all three of his mouths gasping for breath.

It didn't take long for him to go limp. For his mouths to cease moving. He finally stopped laughing and collapsed. Impotent. No more.

She didn't even bother to untie the jacket as she got up. Let him be buried with it, Déjà thought. Let him choke on that "vintage smell" for the rest of eternity.

She recognized the sheets from their video chats. Silky and inviting. Now a fresh piece of raw and defiled piece of meat lay in the center of his bed. She must have imagined Brandon's bedroom a hundred times. What it looked like. What it smelled like. What feelings she would feel if she was lucky to find herself inside of it. She imagined Brandon sweeping her off her feet and carrying her up here so they could make passionate love until sunrise.

"You'll never have to worry about anything again, Déjà Seawright. You're with me now. You're a star."

But what she never would've imagined would be the framed photograph of Richard Nixon he kept on his nightstand (WTF?) or the buckets of gooey semen he kept piled along the wall or the freestanding hydraulic chamber that sat next to the armoire, large enough for him to step into, of course, where his jellyfish-infused body could be pressed back into the same fit and familiar shape it once took in his youth, like the plastic mold Mattel used to make Ken dolls. It was, in essence, a Brandon Bowers-making machine.

But even if a pile of jeweled rubies were sitting in front of her, she would've paid them no more mind than she did any of this other crap. Her focus was solely on the window ahead, where the glorious hills of Hollywood unfurled. Outside. Freedom. So goddamn close.

"Charlie. Oh my god, the bitch killed Charlie."

Marybelle was at the end of the hall. Brandon was not far behind. There was no time to waste. Déjà had seconds before they burst into the room.

She snatched up the cum-covered steak from out of the folds of Brandon's bedspread and threw it as hard as she could through the windowpane. It shattered.

"This way. Brandon. She's in your room. C'mon."

Shards like fangs protruded from the top and bottom of the frame. Her salvation was only one leap of faith away. It was now or never.

So she ran.

She jumped.

And through the air she fell, out into the sprawling night, her landing be damned.

CHAPTER EIGHT

SECOND SKIN II: THE RECKONING

(2019)
DIR. BY TED SPADER JR.

" . . . and so we have the once-great Brandon Bowers, now settling into his final form—an aging, low-rent action 'hero' starring in yet another half-baked European tax-shelter production, destined to land straight-to-the-bowels of Amazon Prime. A more dignified actor in his position would've graduated into more of the 'elder statesmen' or 'boardroom' type roles. The mentor. The CIA director. The old pro showing the hot young rookie the ropes. Etc. But not for Bowers, who clearly still demands top billing. One gets the impression while watching this largely unnecessary sequel that Bowers will never allow himself to play second fiddle onscreen, even to the detriment of his own career. There will never be a Best Supporting Actor nomination for this Leading Man. And while there may still be a director or project out there that can perhaps breathe some new life into Bowers, and give him and his career a second wind, he has yet to find it. Second Skin II: The Reckoning is yet another whiff in a long line of whiffs for the once enigmatic star . . . "

"**F**OR THOUGH THE *righteous may fall, they will rise up again, as the wicked will stumble to ruin when calamity strikes.*"

Proverbs 24:16, Déjà recalled, not because she found the quote particularly resonant, but because she'd heard it repeated at her so many times throughout her life. Proverbs. The Book of Everyday Wisdom. Her mother would reference it often. An excerpt for every occasion, or so it seemed, and when teenage Déjà was acting up and acting out, there was never a shortage of circumstances where her mother felt some esoteric biblical advice might be applicable. Déjà would roll her eyes and let the words wash over her, all the *thees* and *thous* and *thines* and *thouseths,* too dense and dogmatic to try and decipher. And why would she bother, anyway? Déjà didn't need advice. Déjà didn't need control. The walls she was butting up against were put in front of her by other people, her mother included. *"He who is not with Me is against Me."* Matthew 12:30. Déjà needed to express herself. Déjà needed to get out of Eau Claire and be free.

She jumped out the window. Glass cut through her skin as easily as knives cutting through butter, a latticework of little red slits covered her arms and legs and everywhere, deep enough to bleed.

The air was calm and the surrounding streets were quiet. City lights encroached from the bottom of Nichols Canyon, but they barely touched the darkness above. Clusters of stars sat in the sky, impossibly thick. The universe was vast. Empty yet full. Beautiful yet terrifying.

How did I get here? she briefly thought. *What does any of this mean?*

And then she hit the ground.

Hard.

And her right ankle snapped.

Fibula sticking out sideways. White bone erupting through tan skin. Blood pouring out of the fresh wound in viscous squirts. She tried not to look but couldn't help herself. How much blood could she possibly have left in her?

Déjà lay in the grass, stifling her screams by sinking her teeth into her lower lip, only allowing herself a few short seconds to process and overcome the pain.

The driveway bisected the front yard like a river. When she first arrived, the lawn appeared plush and palatial and wonderfully picturesque. Now it stretched out in front of her in an impractical expanse. Nobody needed this much lawn. Nobody needed a house so big they could hide an entire labyrinth in the basement.

The distance between where she was and the gate was formidable. But she hadn't come this far just to give up now. Let her break her other ankle. Let her break every bone in her body. She still had to stand up. She still had to *try*.

Déjà forced herself to her feet. Pain tightened its vice grip. She pushed her way through it. Her vision was blurry with tears.

Putting her weight on her good foot, she took her first step, arms out like a balancing pole, barely able to keep herself upright.

Her second step was more of the same—wobbly and dubious, but at least she was headed in the right direction, toward the gate, toward the street, toward the city, toward the moon. Anywhere but back into this house.

And where were Brandon and Marybelle, she wondered? Did they hear the glass break? Were they still coming after her? Did they know where she wa—

BWWWAAAAAAAA

An inhuman bray nearly toppled her over as a psychedelic display of tail feathers fanned out in front of her, a hundred fiendish eyes suddenly staring her down.

STARLET

One of the peacocks roaming the property blocked her path. Neck bobbing. Beak snapping. Wings out. Warbling and wailing. She remembered what Brandon said about them being territorial. The animal came at her with all of its fury, aggressive, assertive, and clearly pissed off.

But Déjà was pissed off too, and her reaction was as immediate as it was instinctual. Wrath met wrath, primal and unplanned. This peacock popped up out of nowhere, and in response, she punched it in the face as hard as she could.

The bird took the hit, nearly spinning around 180° before falling over, unconscious. A knockout blow from the One-Handed Wonder herself.

More peacocks closed in. She clenched her fists. *It's pheasant season, motherfuckers*, she thought. She was ready to fight the whole flock if need be.

But one by one, the peacocks stood down. Gazes were averted and they allowed her to pass. An injured animal was a dangerous animal. Even the birds knew this. And Déjà Seawright was bleeding and broken and had very little left to lose.

The peacocks retreated and dispersed and she lowered her duke, the Undisputed Featherweight Champion of the World.

After a few agonizing minutes, Déjà finally made it to the end of the driveway but found the gate sealed shut with a magnetic lock. She stomped her good foot on the pavement, hoping to trigger some kind of sensor or pressure point that would open it up automatically. When that didn't work, she tried squeezing her slender body through the bars, but they were so close together she couldn't even get past her elbow. Afraid of getting stuck, she pulled herself out.

"No!" Déjà shook the bars in frustration, a useless

gesture. Unless some code was input into the callbox on the street or a release button was hit from inside the house, this thing was staying shut. "No. No. No. Let me out! Let me out of here!"

A rustle from the bushes on the other side, almost as if in response. But it wasn't the wind. Something was moving around in the sagebrush nearby.

A man groggily stepped out—skinny, sickly, clad in the most obnoxious Tommy Bahama print Déjà could imagine.

Benny!

His fancy over-outfitted camera still dangled from a strap by his side. He stretched. Yawned. Rubbed the sleep out of his eyes.

"Alright, alright, I'm leaving, hold your horses . . . " He nearly tripped over backward at the sight of her. "Oh jeez lady, you scared the shit outta me."

"Benny?! Benny, it's me! It's Déjà! Help me! Please help!"

"Déjà?" He squinted. "Holy shit, I barely recognized you. You're cut to ribbons. And what the hell happened to your hand?"

"Benny, you gotta help me get outta here." Her paranoid eyes darted quickly around. "They're coming."

"Who's coming?"

"They're not human anymore!"

"What?"

"Brandon. Marybelle. Charlie Eccentric. That doctor from the bus stop ads. Even the fucking maid. All of 'em."

Benny, on instinct, hip-aimed his camera in her direction, index finger on the shutter button, ready to shoot, should a photo-op reveal itself. "I'm sorry, what is this about the maid now?" he asked.

"They're killing people, Benny. They've been doing it for a long time. Brandon and his friends are injecting themselves with jellyfish DNA and luring aspiring young actresses into his mansion so that they can torture them and harvest their adrenal glands for drugs."

STARLET

"I think you might be bleeding out . . . "

"Open the gate, Benny. Please."

"I can't," he said.

"You *can't*?"

"I—I don't know the code."

"Shit," she huffed. "Do you have a phone on you, at least?"

"Yeah. Obviously. Who doesn't keep their phone on them?"

"Call the police. Call the National Guard. Call the fucking *National Inquirer* if you got to. Just call someone . . . "

"Yeah, Benny, why don't you call the police." A familiar voice came up behind her. She could hear his footsteps, confidently walking across the pavement. And when Brandon laid his heavy hand on her shoulder, she froze like a deer caught in the path of an oncoming train. "Go ahead, Benny. Call the fuckin' pigs. I've been meaning to tell them about this stalker I've seen lurking around outside my place, anyway. A greasy paparazzo with bad boundaries and an even worse sense of style. '*He's been harassing me for years, officer. I'm honestly concerned for my safety.*' And while they're beating you down with their batons, I'll be snapping selfies with them for their Instagram feeds. '*You'll never guess who I met at work, honey,*' they'll say to their spouses that night as they're climbing into bed. It'll be a story they tell to impress their coworkers and kids. To serve and protect someone like Brandon Bowers? Hell, it's probably as close to greatness as they'll ever come. I'm sure that is something you can understand, isn't that right, Benny?" Brandon motioned toward the camera. "Folks like you. Normal folks. All you can ever hope for is the smallest of sips from the fountain at which I drink every day. That is why you pay attention to people like me. That is why I'm *interesting*. But I am a benevolent man. I know how lucky I am. I appreciate my fans. I appreciate my position of influence. And so I provide. I am the ecosystem, Benny.

You're just a sycophant. So go ahead and call the cops, but just know that you'll only be hurting yourself in the end. And if you're concerned about our little Déjà here, don't be. She's fine. She merely took a bad hit of acid, is all. She's just having herself a good old-fashioned psychedelic freakout. We've all been there, right? Nothing some orange juice, a couple of band-aids, and a nice night's sleep won't cure."

"A bad hit of acid?" Benny was incredulous. Déjà squirmed in Brandon's claw-like grasp. The A-lister dug his fingers deeper into her shoulder.

"Yeah," Brandon replied. "A *really* bad hit."

Marybelle Ashton appeared next to Déjà, intertwining their arms together like a pair of snakes, preventing Déjà from struggling any further or running away.

Benny watched the three of them with grim fascination, a puzzled expression on his face, like he was trying to solve some sort of math problem in his head.

"Something about this doesn't feel right," the photographer eventually said.

Brandon let go of Déjà. Marybelle's grip grew firmer to compensate.

"2-2-1-4," Brandon said.

"What?" Benny replied.

"2-2-1-4," Brandon said again as his gaze flicked to the callbox. "That's the code. Why don't you come on inside? I know that's what you've always wanted, isn't it? To see what was on this side of the gate? So here's your chance. Come in and we'll see if we can't reach some kind of . . . *understanding*."

"The hell're you doing, Bowers?" said Marybelle.

Brandon hushed his *Eggs with a Side of Hope* costar with a wave of the hand.

Benny didn't move. He looked from the callbox, to Déjà, to Marybelle, and back to Brandon again, who raised an innocuous eyebrow.

"No." Benny shook his head. "No, I think I'm gonna stay right here."

STARLET

He lifted his camera up to his eye. Framed them in the viewfinder. Focused his shot. For a moment, panic flashed across Brandon's face, but he quickly regained control, returning to the same cavalier mien he so often wore on the silver screen.

"Okay, fine. Whatever you like. But before you press that little button there, lemme ask you this, Benny: What do you think the open market would fetch you for a photograph of me and Marybelle VERY CLEARLY HELPING this no-name actress who ALSO VERY CLEARLY had herself a little accident?"

"What?"

"C'mon, Benny. How much would, say, celebrityseatsniffer.com pay you for a shot like that? Top number. Let's hear it."

"I don't know . . . maybe something in the ballpark of . . . $10 grand or so . . . "

"$10 grand!" Brandon exclaimed as he reached into his back pocket and pulled out a checkbook and a pen. "These clickbait sites don't fuck around, do they? Damn."

He scribbled out a personal check for $10,000, paid to the order of Benjamin Templesmith. Signed the bottom in the same sloppy script he'd signed a million autographs before it. He held the small rectangle of paper through the bars.

"Go ahead. Take it," Brandon said. "Like I was telling you, we were just having a party and things got a bit out of hand. Our sweet Déjà imbibed a bit too much and got hurt, but we're cleaning her up, as you can see. All in all, it's just another perfectly normal, perfectly harmless night up here in the Hills, wouldn't you agree?"

Benny took the check and ran his finger across the number. $10 large. More money than he'd ever seen at one time in his life.

"Benny . . . " Déjà begged the paparazzo for mercy with her eyes. Brandon shot her an angry look before his steely gaze returned to Benny, awaiting his reply.

"Ah jeez, Mr. Bowers, that's awfully generous of you. And I totally get where you're coming from. Can't fault someone for having a little fun, can I? It's important to unwind at the end of the day. Believe it or not, my job's got its own set of stresses too—which is to say that while $10 grand is certainly a lotta money, it'd be even *nicer* to not hafta worry about my next paycheck either, ya know? I got kids, after all, and I hear college ain't cheap."

Brandon smirked. "You are one slick little worm, aren'tcha Benny?"

"Hey, man. Never take the first offer. That's showbiz, right?"

The photographer winked. Brandon laughed.

"Fair enough. So how about this: Keep the check. Take yourself out to a nice pancake breakfast. Order extra bacon. Live a little. My treat. And from here on out, let's say once a month, you swing by, and I'll let you take a picture of me you can sell to the gossip blogs or supermarket rags or wherever it is you peddle your wares. It'll be something *exclusive*. Something embarrassing even, if you want. Whatever is gonna getcha the biggest payday. Tit-for-tat, Benny. Some mutual backscratching."

Benny gave it a moment of thought. Not a long moment. Just enough to make Brandon sweat. "How about we make it every other week?" he countered.

"Once every three weeks?" Brandon countered back. "And we adjust the timeline as need be if I'm away on a shoot."

"That works for me," Benny said. "But I also get one nip-slip from Marybelle too."

"What?!" Marybelle barked.

"Just one and done?" Brandon asked.

Benny nodded in the affirmative. Brandon turned to Marybelle Ashton who rolled her eyes and acquiesced. "Ugh. Fine. ONE. And we coordinate ahead of time so I can make sure they're looking their best. I don't want one of those schlubby candid beach pics where I'm looking all fat coming out of the ocean, wave knocking a boob loose from my bra."

"Deal," said Benny.

"Great!" Brandon clapped his hands. "Consider it done."

"Benny! Benny, you fuckin' asshole!" Déjà shouted as Marybelle forcibly dragged her toward the house. She didn't put up much of a fight. She barely had any fight left. Her worthless screams were lost among the chorus of peacocks, ululating in the night.

The last thing Déjà saw before she disappeared back into the mansion was Brandon messing up his own hair and bending over awkwardly to pick up the newspaper, the slightest peek of a plumber's crack cresting out of his waistband. He still looked billboard handsome, just slightly disheveled.

The sound of a camera shutter could be heard.

"Oh yeah. Perfect," said Benny as he snapped the picture. "*US Magazine* is gonna gobble this shit up. Brandon Bowers has to pick up his own newspaper?! Wow! Celebrities—They're Just Like Us!"

The door slammed shut. The deadbolt slipped into place. Brandon entered the house, not 30 seconds after Marybelle and Déjà, grumbling to himself as he opened the auxiliary closet to the left of the foyer. He dug through the crap inside for something in the back.

In the living room, Marybelle tossed Déjà onto the sectional leather sofa, a graciously soft landing compared to the last few she had. She sunk into the cushions like they were made of quicksand. Once again, she thought about how easy it would be to just close her eyes and succumb to sleep.

Marybelle buzzed around her, searching shelves and overturning pillows.

"You got a rope or anything?" she called out to Brandon as she opened the drawer on the coffee table and rifled through. Crystalline coasters for cold drinks. Extra batteries for the remotes. The long and already-loaded syringe Brandon stashed in there at the start of the evening. And though her vision was blurred by both fatigue and tears, Déjà was finally able to make out the writing on the side of it.

DohrniiTox.

"What did you say?" Brandon's voice echoed toward them as he approached.

"Rope," Marybelle repeated. "Or like a bungee cord or something?"

"Why would I have a bungee cord?"

"I don't know. I'm just trying to keep her from running away again."

"Well, it might be a bit tough for her to get anywhere . . . " Brandon stepped into the room carrying a handheld cordless hedge trimmer. He pressed a button on it and the saw-toothed blade whirred to life. " . . . once I chop her fucking legs off."

Déjà's eyes shot wide open. She certainly wasn't falling asleep anymore.

"Help!" she screamed, though it was merely a reflex at this point. There was no one to hear her pleas and no one to care.

Brandon eclipsed the light as he hovered over her, a dark and destructive figure, the Reaper Himself. Déjà writhed beneath him.

"Guess ya still got a little vinegar left in ya, huh?" He jammed his dirty index finger into the wound left by Dr. Fish's adrenaline-milking machine and wiggled it around, scraping the walls. She yelped. When he pulled it out, it was covered in thick gunk. Fresh raw adrenochrome. He stuck it in his mouth.

"Ohhhh fuckkkk-k-k-k-k-k-k," he muttered as he once again came in his pants, an orgasm so volcanic his knees almost buckled.

STARLET

"Lemme get some." Marybelle dropped down and stuck her tongue directly into the hole in Déjà's side. *Slurp, slurp, slurp.* She suckled at Déjà's hemorrhaging adrenal gland like a piglet at its mother's teat.

Déjà tried to pry her off, but Marybelle held tight, making gurgling sounds as she supped, too ravenous to savor the taste.

There was nowhere else to go. Nothing else to do. The torture she'd endured was merely the preamble to this moment. Death had now arrived.

This is all I'm good for, thought Déjà. *All I've ever been good for. All I was ever destined to be.*

Once upon a time she had ambition and drive. Once upon a time she held a reservoir of desire in her heart. She wanted more out of life than her hometown was able to offer. Her friends and family never understood. Nobody ever understood. More than money. More than adulation. More than the passing ephemera that fame might offer. *Creation.* That was what mattered. That was what she'd been chasing her whole entire life. The chance to build something bigger than herself—something that felt like it mattered—so that she could connect to the world in a way that was somehow more authentic. More human. More herself. God never answered these kinds of prayers. And so she stopped praying to Him. She wasn't going to find her answers in the clouds. She moved to Hollywood looking for a different kind of religious experience. One she could call her own.

Marybelle wiped the wine-colored goop from the corners of her lips as she stood up.

Brandon held out the hedge trimmers and eyeballed Déjà's legs. "Maybe I should put a tarp down. This couch was like $13,000."

Déjà moaned and attempted to roll over. Brandon pushed her back into place with his foot.

"Oh I know how it is, little darling," he said. "Believe it or not, I was once like you. I came from nothing myself.

I'm a self-made man. A true American success story. I mean, sure my parents were both well-off, but they weren't *ridiculously* well-off. Just regular well-off. And yeah, okay, I had an uncle that worked as an executive at Paramount, but I still had to audition in the beginning. I wasn't guaranteed shit. I *earned* my seat at the table with hard work. As did Marybelle . . . "

"It's true," said Marybelle. "My uncle only worked for Lionsgate."

"So, you see?" Brandon continued. "The three of us, we're all the same. We've all struggled, in one way or another. I bear the cross of my past. That is the nature of the beast. Every time my agent brings me a new script or offer that doesn't quite feel up to snuff, I think: *if only I had been cast as* Iron Man, *then I would be the most beloved, the highest paid, the king of the mountain, with endless choices at my command.* That is my one big regret. My one big failure. The well from which I draw. I have suffered for my art. And I suffer still."

Marybelle tossed her hands up in frustration. "OH MY GOD are you still harping on that stupid *Iron Man* thing?"

"Shut up," Brandon said to her. "You're always trying to upstage me. Just stop it. I get to do the big end monologue. This is my house."

"You know this kinda shit right here is exactly why Feige hasn't cast you in any of his other Marvel flicks. He can sense the bitterness wafting off of you like rotten cabbage. That's why Cumberbatch got Dr. Strange and Pratt got to lead the Guardians and you're out here shooting *Generic Action Flick Part 17* or whatever."

"I said SHUT UP!"

"And it's this exact same kind of caustic energy that caused *Eggs with a Side of Hope* to bomb too. You thought you were above the material. And the audience could tell, even if they couldn't quite put their finger on why."

"What did I tell you about mentioning that movie around me?"

STARLET

Marybelle was undeterred, this old scab picked anew. "I mean, I was good in *Eggs*. I was really good. And why wouldn't I be? I'm the rom-com chick. That's what I do!"

"Yeah. We know. In fact, that's *ALL* that you do. You clearly didn't have the depth or range to keep up with what I was bringing to the screen."

"Coming from the guy who just starred in *Second Skin II*. Ha. Look, all I'm saying is I didn't have any issues when they cast me alongside Hugh Jackman. Or Vince Vaughn. Or hell, not even me and Helena Bonham Carter in the retrospectively cringeworthy *More Than Friends*. You just don't know how to connect with people, Brandon. That's been your problem from the get-go. You're all style and no substance."

"Fuck you," he said to her. "You think it was easy for me to hit those emotional high notes when I was stuck working opposite a block of wood like yourself?"

"I'm the block of wood?" Marybelle brought an affronted palm to her chest. "I was America's Sweetheart before *Eggs*. You sucked the wind right outta both of our sails. And now look at you, with your not-even-Redbox-worthy drivel."

"At least I'm not doing a *sitcom* on network TV like *somebody* I know," he said. "Though I guess that's probably the only place for an actress of your advanced age to find work these days . . . "

"I'm 43!"

"You're prehistoric!"

The two of them were practically at each other's throats, their argument quickly escalating from verbal barbs to outright yelling, both focused more on each other than on their intended victim, Déjà lying prone and unbound on the couch between them.

The DohrniiTox needle rested amid the junk Marybelle pulled out of the coffee table. With a deep breath, Déjà summoned the very last of her strength and flung herself toward it. Rolling off the cushions, she grabbed the syringe on the way down.

She scrambled to her feet, broken ankle and all, and held the needle threateningly out in front of her like a fencing sword.

"Get back!" she shouted. "Get the fuck back!"

Brandon and Marybelle stopped bickering. Brandon looked at the syringe in her hand. "Whatcha planning to do with that, little darling? Play nurse and give me a shot?"

The needle was an ineffectual weapon at best, and the DohrniiTox inside of it was something Brandon was going to administer to himself anyway. She considered her options and was only able to land on one.

She raised the syringe above her head, threatening to smash it to pieces on the ground instead. This got their attention.

"Whoa, whoa, whoa." Brandon held out his palms. "Let's not do anything rash here . . . "

"Don't do anything rash?" Déjà shouted. "YOU EAT PEOPLE!"

"That's all him." Marybelle pointed at Brandon. "I'm an outspoken vegan, as I'm sure you're well aware. Animal welfare is one of my main passions. Check my Wiki. Plus people are too high in calories. I prefer leaner sources of protein. Legumes and the like."

"You were eating my hand earlier!"

"Well yeah, but it was ethically sourced."

"Put down the hedge trimmers," Déjà commanded.

Brandon complied. He placed the power saw at his feet.

"Okay. Okay, I can see when we're beat. Just gently place the DohrniiTox back on the table and we'll let you walk right on outta here. Isn't that right, Marybelle?"

"Huh? Oh yeah. No fuss, no muss. Water under the bridge."

"We can all go our separate ways," Brandon said to Déjà, speaking slowly, soothingly. "You can go back to Eau Claire. You can continue to live your little life and forget this whole night ever happened. There are plenty of other girls where you came from. Plenty of other *leftover parts* . . . "

Déjà cocked her eyebrow. "What did you say?"

Brandon glowered at her. "Oh c'mon, Déjà. Don't be so naive. I was the executive producer on the thing, for god's sake. A show about hand modeling? Like, really? It exists solely so we can find aspiring young starlets like yourself. These are fertile fields. This was the plan the moment you answered that casting call."

Déjà's jaw fell open. "What are you saying? The entire pilot was a setup?"

"Think about it for a second. *Leftover Parts*. It's not even clever subterfuge. We're hiding in plain sight."

"How many people are in on this?" asked Déjà.

"Enough of 'em to get it done. And the ones that aren't in on it know better than to inquire."

"Selena Gomez?"

"Let's just say she's been to Reno a few times herself."

Déjà felt her body deflate. Brandon gave her a smug smile.

"This thing is bigger than me. Bigger than any one person," he said. "Dr. Fish might be dead, but you're not going to be able to stop us no matter what you do."

"No, perhaps I won't," Déjà said, as she plugged the sharpened end of the needle into the thick of her own thigh. "But I can see you in hell."

And before Brandon or Marybelle could stop her, she pushed the plunger down and injected the full dose of DohrniiTox directly into her system.

A rush.

A beautiful, cacophonous, rapturous rush, like nothing she'd ever felt before. Racing through her bloodstream like rocket fuel and cotton candy as the jellyfish DNA bonded with her own. Warmth spread across her skin. Relief. Perhaps more than relief. Exuberance. Joy. Like she was being tickled from the inside out. Her broken ankle no longer hurt. Her severed limbs no longer throbbed. Her spine stiffened and she shook, hummed, vibrated to a frequency she hadn't been able to tune into before. Higher than any leaf she ever smoked. Higher than any powder that ever went up her nose. She was in another place. A sharper place. She could feel the world around her start to shine.

Déjà looked at her remaining hand. Flexed it and released. Her fingers were made of jelly and her flesh was as compliant as clay. A plastic skeleton overlaid with plastic parts. She could take on new shapes. She could remake her own body. She could smooth over her blemishes and fix all her imperfections. Such power was in her now.

And when she looked at Brandon and Marybelle, she could see that for possibly the first time, they were afraid of her.

"Oh fuck," Marybelle yelped.

Déjà could sense the fear resonating off of the leading lady in black waves as thick as brownie batter. She shoved her gelatinous fist into Marybelle's mouth, knocking loose teeth, tearing out her tongue.

Marybelle gummed at Déjà's wrist, but it did nothing to slow the frenzied ingénue, who shoved her hand deeper. Past Marybelle's throat. Down Marybelle's esophagus. Deeper, until Déjà was rooting around inside Marybelle's torso like it was the last place she'd seen her car keys. She clawed through her stomach lining and tore apart her internal organs until she finally located what she was looking for, the kidney, bean-shaped in her palm, on top of which sat Marybelle's swollen adrenal gland, flooding her rapidly expiring body with adrenaline. Déjà could smell it, sweet and enticing.

And when Déjà pulled the kidney free from the tendrils and tendons that held it in place, Marybelle collapsed on the floor. Her heart rate slowed as she choked on her own ruined face. Even biological immortality stood no chance against grievous bodily harm. She writhed for a just few more moments before she fell forever still.

STARLET

Déjà leaned her head back and wrung the kidney out into her open mouth. Purple adrenochrome squirted out of it like soap suds from a sponge, running down her chin as she drank it down in gulps. It stank like raw sewage and tasted much the same, a concentrate of our worst and most animalistic urges. But Déjà quaffed until she could quaff no more, until her palate was saturated and her thirst was quenched.

The full potential of the DohrniiTox now blossomed inside her. What felt like a rush minutes ago had merely been a prelude. She was on another wavelength entirely. Standing up straighter. Puffing her chest out further. Déjà felt unstoppable. No wonder these celebrities were addicted to this shit.

Yet even as she ascended in her mind from a bit player to the main character, it was still not quite enough to physically outmatch Brandon and his imposing Nordic frame. Before Déjà realized what hit her, he had already uppercut her with all his might.

Momentum sent her flying. She tumbled over Marybelle's corpse and fell hard on her back. Her head cracked against the floor and she felt blood soaking in her hair. The pain came flooding back in, more agonizing than ever, and it felt like all the power she'd gained from the Reno instantaneously disappeared. A light switch turned on, and then back off again. A teasing glimpse at divinity before it was stolen away.

She lay there, so dizzy and discombobulated that she could scarcely remember her own name.

Brandon Bowers climbed on top of her, pinning her arms to the ground with his knees. And now his face was sliding off like it was made out of melted wax, taking his hairpiece along with it, landing next to her with a *plop*. His whole body swelled up like it was nothing more than a massive, bubbling tumor. Red varicose veins covered his oily, almost see-through skin. He was more jellyfish than man.

"Get off me!" She thrashed, kicking her feet helplessly up and down, shaking the vases on the end tables around them, rattling the trophy shelf directly above them.

"So you really think you got what it takes, little darling?" He picked up the hedge trimmers and pressed the ON button. She managed to get an arm up and momentarily block him, the gnashing teeth of the garden tool only inches away from eviscerating her. "I have made sacrifices you'll never understand. And I did it not for the glory, but because I am kind. I did it because I am an artist and this is my calling. I did it for you and the millions of other Dorothy Smiths out there just like you, in Eau Claire and Cooperstown and Santa Fe and Annapolis and everywhere. I am an emotional ferryman. I am the mirror of humanity. I am the engine of empathy. I give your lives meaning. That is the job of the actor. That is my noble pursuit. And these things take their toll. These things always demand more. So I give. I give and give and give. Few have the talent and fortitude I have. Few would be willing to give it all like I did. So let me ask you again, Déjà Seawright, do you think you got what it takes?"

She had no leverage. He kept pushing down. The hedge trimmers getting closer, motor screaming as it sucked in the air. And as futile as it was, she continued to fight him. Continued to kick. And every time the floor rattled, Brandon's awards slid further toward the edge of the shelf. Déjà could see the whole array of them, perilously perched, his Golden Globe, his People's Choice, his stupid fucking pathetic fake Oscar, poised like an Olympic diver at the end of a springboard. All it needed was a little push. A little encouragement. A little round of applause. And it would leap.

"A moving speech," Déjà said. "But it's time they played you off . . . "

One last stomp of her foot.

Thump.

And then gravity did the rest.

STARLET

The lead statuette dropped like an anvil. It hit Brandon Bowers directly in the center of his forehead. A crack followed by a sickening, wet squish as it not only pierced his skull, but wedged itself upside down into his brain like a spear. Cerebral fluid sloshed out of the wound as thick as marmalade.

He immediately stopped fighting and his endlessly-erect penis finally waned. The trimmers fell silent. A line of drool ran out of his slackened mouth. He looked at Déjà, his melted face melted even more as he tried to smile one last time.

"Roll credits," he slurred as if drunk. And then he too was gone.

CHAPTER NINE

STARLET

(POST-PRODUCTION, RELEASE DATE TBA)
DIR. DÉJÀ SEAWRIGHT

" . . . *although there is a lot to be proven still in terms of the box-office, early word seems to indicate that first-time writer/director/star Déjà Seawright shines like The Pleiades as the eponymous* Starlet. *Surely, this is a debut performance to be held alongside the greatest in film history: Orson Welles in* Citizen Kane, *the kid who played McLovin in* Superbad, *and of course, the late great Brandon Bowers in* The Perfect Gentleman *who, alongside former costar Marybelle Ashton and pop-artist Charlie Eccentric, was found dead in his Nichols Canyon mansion, the apparent victims of a home invasion gone awry, the result of which put the Tate murders to shame. Ironically, Déjà Seawright herself was present at the same party, and while details are still scarce, she remains the only survivor of that grisly ordeal . . .* "

OWL HOOTS HAD been replaced by the chirps of blackbirds and wrens. The sun was coming up for the day as Benny Templesmith finished packing his equipment. This sagebrush outside the Bowers Estate had been his home away from home for months as he patiently kept an eye peeled for an opportunity to arise like the one that arose last night. $10,000 in his pocket, with the indefinite promise of more. As a paparazzi he knew, you only had to wait these people out. That sooner or later, they'd slip up, and then it'd be his time to shine. Perhaps you could call it extortion, but Benny wasn't the bad guy here. Whatever was going on beyond those gates, that was the real horror show. Fame does something to a person. It changes them. And these celebrities, from what Benny could surmise, were not like you and me. It wasn't his place to try and figure them out. To decipher their motives. To judge their behavior. He was merely an observer. And he had to eat too.

But just before he left, there came a sound. Lopping. Slow. Rhythmic. Getting closer. Somebody was walking up.

From out of the shadow of the mansion, Déjà materialized, as if she were a ghost coming back to haunt him. All the peacocks parted for her. The mourning doves went silent too. She was bloodier and more broken than she'd been a mere 20 minutes earlier when Brandon and Marybelle dragged her back inside. But that wasn't her blood she was covered in, he realized. The house in the background had fallen still.

She reached the end of the driveway. Benny was too afraid to even move. With a quick nod of the head, she motioned to the callbox. He gulped. Leaned over to it.

2-2-1-4.

The gate swung open.

"Ms. Seawright, listen . . . " he started to say, but the

127

look she gave clammed him up quick. Though barely over five feet tall, in that moment Déjà towered over him like the Statue of Liberty. In her gaze he felt as helpless as a baby, as insignificant as an ant.

She reached out and took his bag from him. Benny released it without protest. She pulled the camera out, gave it a quick inspection, then pointed it at the photog and clicked the button. It made a shutter sound. His picture appeared on the screen on the back, washed out by the flash, capturing this moment, freezing him in it.

"What did I tell you before, Benny? No fucking comment."

And Déjà dragged her battered body down the twisted side streets. Taking random turns and cutting through yards until she eventually found Nichols Canyon Road. Toward the east, the black of night was already yielding. Golden rays of light came up over the horizon.

Down the winding hill. The surrounding multi-million-dollar properties getting smaller and smaller behind her as she went, not even a mile away from where she started, and yet already, she was in an entirely different world. The topography quickly transformed, taking on the familiar grid pattern of the Valley, but now on the other side of the mountain. The Hollywood side. And here she was, hitting Hollywood Boulevard, and swinging a left, shuffling down the palm tree-lined sidewalk on her broken ankle, leaving gory footprints with every lugubrious step.

Whatever charge she'd gotten from the DohrniiTox and adrenochrome was long spent. She now felt even more tired and more beaten up than she ever had before.

And still, she continued on, exhausted. dehydrated, swollen with jellyfish slime.

People were waking up. Commuting to work. Walking their dogs. Tourists were already out, getting an early start,

STARLET

trying to beat the crowds. She was drawing attention to herself. She could see groups of people stopping to stare, a curious kind of horror on their collective faces. Was this some kind of joke? A setup? Was a movie being filmed right now?

There were famous landmarks along the way. The ones she always associated with Los Angeles. Madame Tussauds. Grauman's Chinese Theater. The Capitol Records Building up ahead at the intersection of Vine. And beneath her, the most iconic landmark of all, where the sidewalk had been replaced by the Walk of Fame.

Déjà fell to her knees. She could force herself forward no longer. Her body gave out. And she lay there, bleeding upon the star-spangled street, surrounded by the names of all her favorite celebrities, those who came to this town before her, those who literally paved her way. These were people she felt more kinship to than her friends. Then to even her own family. Perhaps these people didn't know she was out there, liking their photos on Instagram and filling up the theaters each time one of their movies premiered, but that would soon change. Like Brandon said, to make it in this industry you had to be ready to sacrifice everything. Déjà already made her peace with that fact a long time ago.

In the distance, an ambulance. The sound of sirens bouncing across the pavement. Getting louder and louder. Coming to save her.

She was the final girl. And this was her final scene.

Dozens of people had gathered around her at this point. Gawking. Gabbing. Holding up their cellphones to take pictures and videos. Sharing her face on TikTok and Twitter. A news van arrived. Reporters joined the mix. All eyes in her direction. All cameras pointed her way. Her teeth were still miraculously intact. Her dark eyes retained their sincere sparkle. And before she passed out, she gave her adoring public a wide and welcoming smile.

Hello Hollywood, she thought. *My name is Déjà Seawright and I have arrived.*

ACKNOWLEDGEMENTS

Thanks to the following people who have helped me and my career throughout the years in ways both big and small: Constance Ann Fitzgerald. Bubbles the Cat. Tank the Dog. John Skipp. Rose O'Keefe. Matt Blairstone. Alex Woodroe. Michael Allen Rose. Karmen Wells. Daniel Barnett. Eirik Gumney. And others I'm forgetting because it's like 1 AM right now.

Big thanks to Max Booth III and Lori Michelle and Ghoulish Books for enabling my weirdness and continuing to publish me.

And of course, thank you to Armie Hammer. Why won't you reply to my DMs?

ABOUT THE AUTHOR

Danger Slater is the Wonderland-Award winning author of *I Will Rot Without You, Moonfellows, He Digs a Hole*, and other books too. He has a mustache. Or maybe he shaved it by now. Or maybe he is already dead. I don't know when you're reading this.

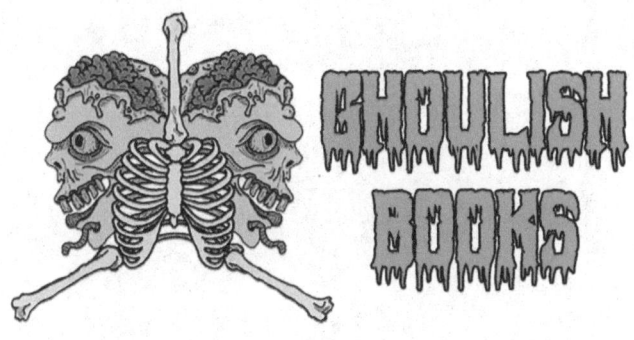

Patreon:
www.patreon.com/ghoulishbooks

Website:
www.Ghoulish.rip

Facebook:
www.facebook.com/GhoulishBooks

Twitter:
@GhoulishBooks

Instagram:
@GhoulishBookstore

Linktree:
linktr.ee/ghoulishbooks

Patreon:
www.patreon.com/ghoulishbooks

Website:
www.Ghoulish.org

Facebook:
www.facebook.com/GhoulishBooks

Twitter:
@GhoulishBooks

Instagram:
/at/ghoulishbooks.com

LinkTree:
linktr.ee/ghoulishbooks